THE SECOND SEASON
OF
JONAS
MacPHERSON

THE SECOND SEASON OF JONAS MacPHERSON

LESLEY CHOYCE

THISTLEDOWN PRESS

Canadian Cataloguing in Publication Data

Choyce, Lesley, 1951-
    The second season of Jonas MacPherson

    ISBN: 0-920633-67-6

I. Title.
PS8555.H693S4 1989   C813'.54   C89-098071-3
PR9199.3.C569S4 1989

Book design by A.M. Forrie
Cover painting by Carol Fraser

Printed and bound in Canada by
Hignell Printing, Ltd., Winnipeg

Thistledown Press Ltd.
668 East Place
Saskatoon, Saskatchewan
S7J 2Z5

Acknowledgements

Excerpts of this novel have previously appeared in:
event, Canadian Fiction Magazine, Coming Up for Air (St. John's: Creative Publishers,
1988).

Special thanks to my wife Terry and to Malcolm Ross. Both provided valuable advice
and criticism in the preparation of this novel.

This book has been published with the assistance of The Canada Council and the
Saskatchewan Arts Board.

For my grandmother, Minnie.

Going from the past to the present and back was like walking into and out of different rooms. I only had to be careful that a draft didn't steal up and close the door behind me. I could walk around inside this temporal house almost at will and was comfortable in any room I had once occupied. I recognized the dangers, or at least I thought I did. But the rewards were too great to give it up.

CONTENTS

_____ **Inheritance**

At sixty-nine I am an arrogant old son of a bitch and the ocean is my mistress. She keeps me sane. She keeps me alive. Science has never convinced me that the sea is not a fully developed conscious entity. Living here on my battered hillside, my abbreviated drumlin, I have been engaged in a spiritual arm wrestling with the North Atlantic for most of my life. She's been hard on my real estate. She's murdered off more of my people than World War II and, at times, she has bullied me into believing that the world lacks any semblance of compassion. She has taught me rage. Here on the coast, our hearts are sometimes like stiff, rock-hard muscles squeezing the life from each other. I am egotistical enough to believe that the fight is a personal one, that the Atlantic cares whether I breathe or die. It wants me to live, to see the final hurricane rip a cave deep into the meaty thighs of the cliff, to undercut the foundation, to send me—house, teakettle, and tempered brain—crashing to the knuckled rocks below. This pugilistic sea has been waiting for the fight since it first cooled its belligerent youth in the boiling adolescence of the planet. She

saw me coming when the retreating glacier dropped this nob
of mud and rock to shed its skin northward and forever drool
its life out into her throat.

The grass is still jungle green, barbered low by a scythe and
a bent back, an old man stooped with cantilevered arms
pumping away in the August heat, a thin impotent fog hovering off the shore as always. Turn your back and it sneaks up
thick around your wrists and steals the very light from your
windows. August is not to be trusted in Nova Scotia. Expect
frost after the Sunday of a blinding sun. Expect the sea to
conjure up a damp summer sun and short pants on Christmas.
Expect April to bring the worst arctic onslaught of the year.
No month is to be trusted.

The sea has teased us here, snaking its Gulf Stream tongue
off toward Iceland and Europe just beyond the lips of the
shoreline. It takes the artillery of a tropical storm to slap warm
water on our shores but even then, only at the expense of a
dozen barns and magnificent grief to the Power Corporation.

But you must not see me, Jonas MacPherson, as a bitter old
man. Sixty-nine is not old. Behind me is only youth and ahead,
eternity. I exist exquisitely at the very centre of time. It fades
endlessly into the past and trickles infinitely far into the
future. In truth, I have found that I can be profoundly old or
vigorously young.

A man came by with a transit—a surveyor half my age. He
treated me with great deference, with respect and a slow,
diligent speech. I felt like a revered and sacred stone monu-
ment; centuries stood between us. Inside, something glazed
and cracked and my voice warbled like I had heard other old
men's do.

He meant well, he was wondering about the shoreline. How
far had my drumlin once intruded into the sea? He called it
a "drummond", however. They both mean the same thing, this
hill of glacial drift. You can still hear the glacier scraping and
clawing its way back north in the night. It sleeps in the rocks
and when they sweat in the cool heat of summer basements,

they leak the noise into our ears, a shrill, sometimes rasping song set against the garrulous orchestration of stones washing back and forth in the waves at the base of the cliff.

"The hill stretched clear to Africa," I told the surveyor. It was not what he wanted to hear. But I often thought it to be true. The hill appears unfinished. It breaks off even as it sweeps gracefully upward. I envision that somewhere on the other side, in Morocco or Senegal, the geography is completed. The hill, a graceful sweep of green where men remain more primitive, more happy than us. I was polite. I offered this surveyor, this man who made me feel as old as the stones, some tea, some home-made beer. He politely declined. The world might move on without him. His time was not the time of an old man. I told him nothing of the three fallen outhouses, of the loss of more than a foot this very year, and the other, older house that had long since tumbled into the sea and gone looking for the companionship of shipwrecks on the outer ribs of the continental shelf.

On other days, I am still a child waiting to grow up. A teenaged girl in torn blue jeans and flannel shirt arrived late one morning, poking around the perimeter of my field. Looking for old bottles, old keys, old hinges, old things of rust and value. She saw me walking toward her and smiled, turning me instantly into a boy of nineteen. I was shy. I blushed. She showed me a turn-of-the-century perfume bottle that she found. This alone was impossible. As far as I knew, no woman, save my wife, had ever lived here on this hill and the bottle could not possibly have been Eleanor's.

"I didn't know anybody lived up here," she said. So many people said that. The world had forgotten that I was here. From a distance, my house looks untended, empty. I keep it that way, except for the scythe-mowed grass.

"I do, but you're welcome here," I told her as she unearthed a capped rum bottle that was somewhat familiar to me. "My father owned stock in the company," I told her. And she laughed. Her hair, her eyes danced. We had nothing more to say to each other.

"Happy hunting."

"You don't mind?"

"I don't." I would have lopped off both my legs for the opportunity to stand there five more minutes and talk with her, but I was afraid I would lose the fixation that had come over me. The fear of growing quickly old in her eyes. Of broadjumping from nineteen to sixty-nine and beyond in the space of a question, a look. It was too dangerous to take the chance. I would remain a commuter between adolescence and senility. Maybe she would return and we could learn names.

But I have seen old men, once young boys, with callused hands and nervous eyes who have withered into old flesh with flaccid biceps and womanly faces. I am not one of them. When Eleanor died I made a solemn pact with the sea that I could have no more of dying. It is not a thing to be drawn out so that death is allowed to gather such power from the world. It must be concise and orderly. If I am to decide that this very business of being alone, of sleeping in single beds, of making single cups of tea, of talking softly to the flame of a candle—if they are suspected to be the coffin nails of death, I will cancel out any more years of it. But I am convinced that these things are the domain of living and, therefore, I go on. I understand this business of men alone in the world. My father suffered from it. It is not a pretty mural.

But I am not as maudlin as all that. Last night I got drunk and sang Gaelic songs to the three-quarter moon. The sea was lying: it purred along the rocks and tickled ribbons of light across the expanse. The dew washed my bare feet in the cool grass and I could only get a third of the words right in the songs that were both tragic and comic. My father had taught me the words, but even his lyrics were only ever half-right. He was not a Scot, but had been half-raised by an Indian who claimed to be. The Scots, it would seem, were obsessed with things being taken away from them. If we can believe the old songs, to be a Scot was to lose a woman, to lose your land, to lose your livelihood, to lose your very heart in the heat of your self-imposed defeat. My adopted inheritance. I went to set the quart bottle of homebrew on the grassy rim of the cliff and missed. It toppled down the slide and shattered on the boulders below, splashing icicles of glass in the moonlight.

* * *

It's morning and the pigeons are flying. They live in my collection of old cars, all automobiles that I once drove, then gave up on, the way some animals shed skin. They're in the front yard where the sea can't get at them except with her cold salt tongue that stings the paint loose and sucks the rust to the surface. The older ones fare better than the recent vintage. My '46 Chevy is still round and black, bumpers shiny as a recently won war. It houses three pair of rollers and my old mottled homer with the crooked beak.

The pigeons flap out the windows in the morning and collect in the wind like flotsam in a whirlpool; they start out in a tight concentrated circle above the cars, then spiral outward, collecting the rest of the flock as they move up, stealing speed from the thermal wind pumping up the face of the cliff. When they hit some invisible ceiling, they break form. The rollers flip over and over downward and the homers vector out to sea with the urgency of fulfilled instinct. I use binoculars to watch out for chicken hawks and the rare bald eagle. Sometimes the gulls are out for blood as well.

On December 6, 1917, I saw a single giant wave of birds fly east from Halifax like a feathery arm of God sweeping across the sky. My father had been working at the docks. A stevedore, a bent mountain of a man with a back like the Citadel. They had him on a night shift performing oxen tasks in near-blackness through the cold, bleak nights. He came home in time to kiss my mother goodbye as she left to teach school on Brunswick Street. That day, my father was disturbed about something. I was five years old and familiar with the morning changing of the guard. I waited for him to fall asleep. Instead, he picked me up and hauled me out the door without a word. We walked in the direction of the school, up seven steep Halifax blocks, then he cursed through his teeth and changed direction. I can remember, at last, being carried like a length of firewood and hearing the old man's coarse breath like he was fighting for air to breathe. He took me to the harbour and onto the ferry that sat on the water like a worried loon filling up with early morning travellers to Dartmouth. Everything glistened a crystal grey. The sky out toward sea looked heavy and I had never felt such strangeness. We could hear other ships in the harbour, big ships with engines thundering. As if to allow me more air to breathe beneath the forbidding sky, it seemed that my father had himself stopped breathing. I held on tight.

We got off on the old wharf in Dartmouth and this time I was hoisted up onto his shoulders as he made giant strides up Portland Street, still not speaking a word. Outside a grocery story he found a horse-drawn cart, its owner inside with goods for the proprietor. I was set up onto the seat and we were off along the cobbles, neither one of us looking back. I began to feel a great sense of adventure and admiration for my father who had such immediate command over the properties of the world. The sky began to clear as we rose up out of the city and made our way toward Cole Harbour. It was then I saw the great winged arm of God sweeping through the sky. And then came the sound, thunder almost visible in the air. The ground shook and the horse lurched us ahead. My father shook the reins and spoke in Gaelic. In the harbour, the Imo and the munitions ship, Mont Blanc, had collided and ripped the city apart. I held my ears as my father grabbed his own chest with a claw-like hand and wrenched hard on himself, crying out in an inhuman desperate noise that made the horse stop dead in its tracks. The wave of birds passed above us and disappeared silently to the east.

* * *

He left me with an old woman in a place called Keg Harbour. The old woman had loose, flapping skin and wore tight clothes. She smelled of lard and salt fish and hugged me too much from the start. I sat by her cookstove and watched pieces of glowing softwood filter like boiling orange metal through a grate into the grey, dead ashes below, while outside the wind howled, the snow fell. My father had left me there on that distant planet and fled back to Halifax to find my mother who had been standing too close to the large windows on the east side of the school.

I was so young that the memories crowd around a single feeling and are otherwise incomplete. There was this crowding out of all I had known by new, hollow fears. Not exactly fears. Emptiness. I became a giant empty cave. My skin was real, nothing else. The old woman called herself Margaret and talked while she was alone in the kitchen. Others just called her Mar. These were her children, I supposed, grown up and living nearby in the fog and drifting snow. They came by once in a while for favours. "Margaret, just don't complain and do it," she said to herself. She loved these sons and daughters who appeared to have no redeeming qualities whatsoever. There had never been talk of a husband. Margaret split her own wood, salted her own fish, smoked a pipe with a weed in it called kinnickinnick and cursed the weather with more vigour than any person I ever met after her. I was a bit young for it, but she tried to teach me letters; only she made her own S's backwards and K's looked more like H's and she didn't really know how to spell. This I discovered later when I rediscovered my old yellowed pages of foolscap that I had somehow managed to preserve.

But Margaret had long soft, grey-brown hair that fell like sweet, warm fog down her shoulders and hung the length of her broad, rounded back. She would ask me to comb her hair and then she would sing songs that had no words, just syllables. Her singing, more than her stews and chowders, kept me alive through January, February and March and when my father returned on April the third, he looked at me good, then grabbed Margaret and kissed her saying, "Mar, you are the most beautiful woman I could ever imagine." Then she began to cry and she cried for over an hour while she sang songs that sounded sad yet happy, and the fire burnt down to nothing for the first time that winter while outside it still rained cold drool that softened the frozen skin of the earth.

Margaret, even to my eyes, seemed much older than my father. He moved in and slept in the kitchen with me where it took him days and then weeks to try to explain about my mother. But I didn't want to hear about my mother, only about the explosion which seemed a crazy and wonderful thing and I could not connect her death with such an awful and exciting event. By summer, the cave in me had grown smaller but more definite and distinct. Something like a pearl in an oyster had hardened around this vacuum and I carried it like a lump in the throat with me as I walked out over the low tide rocks where I picked up defeated starfish, tricked by the retreating sea and stranded. I carried them back into the waves and let the water sting my feet and cut like icy tourniquets around my ankles.

In those days the sea was clean and blue and green and always full of magical flowing seaweed like dead women's hair attached to the skulls of rocks at the bottom. The tiny things that crawled the cellars of each pool knew my name and told me things I will never forget. They taught me how to borrow light from the sky and steal heat from the coldness of the sea and directed me to highways along the rocks, rocks that sometimes came up to bite at my knees or grab my legs and make me trip, rocks that forgave me of my foolishness as I skipped their sons out to deeper tribes.

I came across a grey seal once, gutted, raw, impossibly grotesque with a belly of wrenched meat. His jaw had been cut out and sent (I learned later) to Ottawa for payment, the fishers being asked by the government to slaughter them at will for a bounty. The seals, it was thought, ate too much fish and spoiled the harvest of the sea.

Elbows and knees made up the most of me. Bony shoulders and ribs. The bones wanted to get out. But when I fell I leaked only blood which tasted salty like the sea and if I cried, that too was some gift from the ocean. There was no sand near, only rock and, for me, the ocean lapped at those rocks and argued among pebbles and slapped hard at the wrists of stone cliffs.

In July, my father cut his hair short with a gutting knife in front of a cracked mirror in Margaret's room. He scraped his face with the same knife, after attending to its edge with a whetstone for what must have been hours. When he held the knife up lengthwise to the sun, it was so sharp that it cut the sunlight in two and divided the world down its sharpened edge. There was some ship to arrive at a harbour down east, one larger than anything that had ever come in there and it was to pick up a few good men, of which my old man was one. They were to go work the Banks for a couple of months and haul the fish to Britain, for the war was still on and men needed food to fight.

When Margaret told me this, she looked younger and thinner than I had known her. I saw then that she had changed while my father had weathered the end of winter in her warmth. She tried to explain how everything would be all right as my father pushed me up to the sandpaper of his face and broke every bone in my body with a hug. He held my arms in the giant clamps of his fists and drove his hard blue eyes deep inside me as he hung on, repeating all the while, "When I'm back, Jonas, when I get back, as soon as I get here, just the moment I can, when you see me again, Jonas . . . "

And he left, of course. All the men were leaving everywhere in those days, hollowing out the families and leaving empty beds and unsplit wood and there was never much of themselves they could leave behind because it took so much to just live and get on with it in those sad, cruel, comical times.

Three days after he had gone, I saw the first automobile I had ever seen around Keg Harbour. Somebody from away, a salesman maybe, or a tourist, although there was hardly such a curiosity in these years. A fool, whoever he was, driving a convertible rig along the headlands and drinking from a bottle. I studied him as he tempted fate, tracing the perimeter of the cliff with the car, then stopping to urinate over the cliff while the engine still ran and the emergency brake let the car slip ever so gently off into old ruts made by bogs and tiny frustrated streams.

Finally he got back into his car and sputtered off toward the west. He saw me, where I stood, out picking foxberries and pigeonberries and he waved, tilted his bottle up to the sky and gave her more gas. He seemed happier than any human being I had ever known and then, suddenly he was gone, his tires straying too near the edge and wanting air beneath their tread rather than rock and sedge. The whole machine went over the side but the man never screamed. It seemed so ludicrous and impossible that I could not believe the man or his car had existed at all. But the fistfight of metal against rock was real enough to convince me. Then it stopped and there were only singing birds, a gentle lapping sea, the lisp of wind in stunted spruce and a queer sensation of calm surrounding the hollow pearl in my chest. Off to the sea, I saw for the first time in my life, two whales spouting water up into the sky, and beyond them a wall of fog held at bay by the offshore breezes.

I scrambled down the cliff and studied the undercarriage of the automobile that lay bleeding gasoline, oils and fluids on the clean round stones. The body of the man had been thrown clear, and miraculously, he seemed complete, only scratched and lumped up as if it were a puppet whose master had let go of the strings. Otherwise, he seemed quite normal and unperturbed. But quite dead. I had always known that life could be stolen from the inside, that it could happen without ripping anything out at all. The evidence was clear.

_____ **Crawling out from Under**

I sit down and write long, elaborate letters to Eleanor. When she died I found it absolutely impossible to believe that anyone else on earth had ever suffered as much as I did. It was inconceivable that my agony had been played out over and over for thousands and thousands of years. When that simple and obvious fact settled in, when I realized that I was not alone, that this simply was the way it worked, the way life ended and the way we carried on, I suspended my belief in the world.

I saw myself as the man whose car had gone off the cliff. I was thrown clear of the wreckage and left to wait for scavengers on the unforgiving rocks. And I let the rocks break my vertebrae one by one, let them gouge in my cheeks and carve out my chest. I sat outside my house on this other cliff and dared the gulls to swoop down and peck out my eyes.

In my childhood, when the authorities had finally found the reckless driver (for I had never told a soul of the tragedy) they said that gulls had found him first, had sniffed out death and ventured in to eat the eyes. The high tide crabs had found their way as well and were at work on his wounds. The sea had

already begun to usurp the body of the car with rust and as
the remains of the owner were hauled off to an inland grave,
the sea was allowed to continue its feast until it was satisfied.

I would not allow a funeral for my wife. I wanted her home
and buried on this hill. Again it seemed impossible that this
was not to be allowed. Some improbable stranger whose eyes
were grey with passivity explained how they were required by
law to push chemicals into the body and bury her in a casket
that would not permit decay of the corpse for many years. I
touched his lapels with one hand and insisted I would bury
my wife properly in a wooden box of my own building in a
grave of my own shovelling, on a piece of land of my own
possession that could only be taken away by the eventual
cravings of the ocean.

"We'll have you arrested," he answered, a voice without any
life at all, a living corpse whose trade was in dead bodies. I had
seen those eyes before in the oldest of herring gulls caught in
nets and resigned to doom. He brushed my hand aside and
walked off.

My letters to Eleanor read quite differently.

So now they give me a year at tops. "Do something with your
life before you're dead," Kenzie tells me. "Just don't sit on your
butt." Kenzie, too, was told by some doctor that he was going
to die. The pronouncement came when he was twenty-nine.
Kenzie is pushing seventy-two now. Pissed the doctor right off,
a fat old Halifax high forehead Tory by the name of Lowden.
Proud of his ability to predict death. Claimed he could look
in your eyeballs and one ear and pin it down to the day of the
week.

But I don't believe that I will die. I don't really think death
is possible. Not for me. Eleanor was too fragile. I knew it when
I married her, a piece of expensive china—not that she was
brought up that way. It was the way I loved her. I formed her
into this terrifyingly fragile thing. I shouldn't have done it. To
the world she was like anyone else, but when I found her and
held her hand, I could feel this something coming out of my
skin and performing art on her, making her into something

too beautiful to be human. I loved her and she is dead. She can touch me yet, but death can not, only its ally the sea. But the Atlantic is no traitor, no henchman, no mercenary; she speaks her own truths full of terror and beauty. She sings sweetness from death and pulls the life apart, pulls the hills apart in the same breath. She never sleeps, she never loves, and, if I'm not careful, we will convince each other we are old friends and break each other's hearts.

One night two months ago I discovered that I could not sleep. The moon was out and I could feel it pulling sleep away from me. I'm not sure I have the capacity any longer. Sure, if you lie long enough alone in sweaty nervous sheets, something happens to your body. Rigor mortis, not sleep. I can live without it. I go out to my pigeons at three o'clock in the morning and stand upright among them. I hear them move, I can feel their hearts beating in the close air. They do not mind and if there are demons in me, my birds are happy to take them from me and, in the morning, soar to fantastic heights and drop the devils to the starving sea, then abandon my sorrows to the winds that carry them back to Europe.

One day before her death, I walked into my kitchen where Eleanor sat with a cup of warm tea steaming in the soft sunlight. Her hair was, like always, falling to her shoulders. I had been mowing the lawn with a gasoline mower and had cut the head off a snake. It made me feel awful, a killer of something important. But I couldn't explain it to her. She saw the blood on my hand. She saw the bite. The head had bitten me, even after it was no longer attached to the body. Eleanor dumped her tea down the sink, poured me a cup, went out and threw the mower over the cliff.

We didn't usually throw things to the sea unless it was hungry and we knew it was hungry for this absurd machine of death. The grass grows tall and green now, turns brown in a puckered sun and falls sideways in the snow. When the ice forms in January, crystal geometry rivets the yard into the hard absolute beauty of cold. To hell with lawnmowers.

If you were to cut off my foot with a lawnmower it would grow back. I am sure of it. The snake did not grow another head, but feet are possible. The doctors can not kill me with their predictions. To name a thing is to use it as a weapon for murder. Kenzie knows this. Kenzie and I could live forever if we had the desire. We are absolutely certain. The frightening thing is that it might happen against our will. My only ally then would be the sea. She'll do me in if the need comes. But I will not want death after a single year.

Kenzie gets drunk and goes epic on me. He believes, in his drunkenness, that he was there at the birth of the sun. "It wasn't as exciting as you would think," he confides. "We were all there," he says, "our molecules packed like crammed commuters on a New York subway and there should have been love but there was too much hate so one day, we were all sent looking for the solar suburbs." This has something to do with physics. Kenzie is a man of science; I am not.

Some days I am so filled with peace, I want someone to find me and say, "This man is a saint." I'm not, of course. When I was fifteen I discovered sex with a girl who smelled of fish and stove oil and when her younger brother found us breaking the seals of life he hit me over the head with a shovel. I got up and nearly killed him with my fists. He was frail and had one leg shorter than the other from birth. I could not forgive myself for nearly killing him and became his best friend against the world. His sister became a nun and lives alone in a small stone room with one high window. Shovels have always acted as aphrodisiacs to me since. The turning of sod remains one of the greatest pleasures of the world.

I wrote off to Winnipeg one year for some birds. More tumblers and rollers. I wanted to see the sky berserk with somersaulting pigeons. They arrived and I went down to the CN to pick up the crate. Half-starved. Shouldn't have trusted railroads to take care of anything living. Paid the young nose-picker his due and then put the birds in the old Rambler to go home. Had the crate been opened, they would have shot out and boomeranged to Manitoba, half-dead, starved senseless. Some image inside their skulls would have flashed alive and fed the wind under their wings till they were there. Most of them.

It could have been some cruel Ukrainian joke that had produced the pair of suicide rollers and sent them east like a postcard from the devil. I didn't know them from the rest. Black and white and splotched, certainly as healthy as the others, no worse, they ate like they believed in living. They were sheltered away with the rest in the burnt-out milk delivery truck, the kind where the driver once had to stand up and drive to save time on deliveries. Two weeks later I let them out. I had faith that they wouldn't flap off west with the company of my own stock handy. And I noticed that one pair hung back until the rest were kissing clouds but then, at last, they flew— spiralling outward in larger concentric circles up toward the mackerel sky, nipping the ceiling, then hanging there suspended like they had hawk blood in them. Then they shot forward together like dancers in a hard-pressed ballet and began to roll. I had never seen such a descent. Over and over, perfectly parallel and in control. That was the worst part. In control to the end. I heard their bodies crack on the flat slab of slate that sits outside my back door. Just like that. Determined, programmed and successful in their override of life. Bred to perfect suicidal perfection, they had been born with the mandate to snap their necks in two when they first found freedom. A letter arrived two days later from the pigeon dealer in Winnipeg. Sorry, he said, he had made a mistake and sent along two suicide rollers in the batch. "Don't let them out whatever you do. Keep them for show. Very expensive birds." He wouldn't charge me an extra cent, he said. His error. Business was growing so.

Chemistry and biology. We're victims of them both. I get tired of thinking about it. I want life, spirit. So much blood is shed in the name of reason, it founders as worthless against the darker half of irrationality. Sit in the dirt in June and fondle the feathered carrot tops poling about in the air for life, watch the fiddleheads burst out of a winter prison as they uncurl a gentle fist in the damp green spring air, study the plain and dismal field asters that look like worthless weeds all summer until near frost when they pollute the world with exotic blue flowers in defiance of all that brown. All around me, people are shovelling graves for the living. I will have none of it.

*   *   *

Carey, my only son, was a good boy. He worked hard at making himself unhappy and this worried me. He had the ambition of an American and I tried to weed that out of him with love. Eleanor didn't quite see ambition to be the disease that I knew it to be, but then Eleanor was fragile beyond the pull of ambition. Carey did better in school than I wanted him to. He was embarrassed by me sometimes, I know, ducking down under the dash in the old Plymouth coupe as we drove into town and some classmate in a newer car passed us on the left. Carey was afraid he'd grow up to be like me, a contented old fart without a mortgage or a civilized job and not a debt in the world.

As soon as he could, he got the train and went to Toronto. Made money. Sold insurance. I hated insurance—bleeding money out of people, encouraging them to plan for death. No living man should ponder his own corpse, let alone the quality of the box that it should be stored in. I tried not to criticize in my letters. He kept going to school, often a bad sign. University courses in business administration. Night school toward an MBA. He was trying so hard, I knew he couldn't be happy. And then he cracked and the government had to pump drugs into him for a month until they said he was better. So he went back to plotting how to sell more policies until one November afternoon when firemen had to haul him down off the CN Tower. He was ready to jump but he didn't. He was scared. That saved him.

I left Eleanor alone for the first time in my life and went to Toronto by plane. I didn't tell her what had happened. I slept on Carey's couch and listened to his jazz records with him. We drank beer and played checkers. He cheered up. He told me

what a wonderful place Toronto was and took me to restaur-
ants where people looked at me funny while Carey pretended
he didn't care. He had started smoking and was nervous,
skittery, talked about sports which I knew nothing about. I
wanted to give him a hug but it was beyond me. He lived alone.
He didn't understand touch, and words were things used to
persuade. Carey convinced me he was doing about as well as
anyone else in the world. He didn't really mind any longer
that he wasn't happy. He would get back to his studies,
continue up the ladder of the job. It was something to stuff
into life, to fill it up, to make it appear to work.

   Later that Christmas, he sent me a large wooden crate full
of glossy magazines with pictures of half-naked women, advertisements for expensive booze and cars and hi-fis. He thought
I needed something new in my life. He had been saving these
for me, he said. I didn't show them to Eleanor. Imagine
spending so much time looking at the flesh of people you have
never met. I caulked up the box exquisitely. Then I painted it
red and, at the highest tide of the spring, I hauled the crate
out to the point and heaved it seaward where the stiff rip would
pull it out so that the northwest wind would shove it someplace
else. It floated. Maybe the right person would find it. Or maybe
it would sink.

                              * * *

You wake up on a morning in February in the middle of your
life and the house is cold. You feel it clinging to the skin of
your face and burrowing into the sockets of your nose. Two
impersonal arms of emptiness are crawling up from the foot
of the bed and the cold is injecting itself into your feet. And
then you are awake in a thin grey light that has nothing to do
with living. You want to retreat back into the narcotic of sleep
but a warm hand has found its way to you and it strokes your
back. You turn and find another body, softer than yours and
giving, pulling you toward it. Outside the wind chants on,
wringing melody from thundering waves and staging sad
choruses with the spruce tops. It bends and lilts around the
walls of the house and wails cacophonous soprano arias in

through the shortcomings of your construction. It is not to be feared. Winter retreats quickly from this secured space as the woman builds her armies of love around you and fills you with the perfect excitement of being alive. Awake for another day, triumphant against the storm, the coastal ravaging, the apocalypse of the Nova Scotia winter.

Eleanor brings me back to the living with her tongue in my mouth and the touch of her hand drawing angels in the small of my back. We are the two most important human beings on the face of the earth and our bodies endorse the fact. My love in its comic rigidity and hers in its infinite softness conspire to dance heat into the house. Age has changed nothing. Nothing at all. Afterwards, Eleanor falls back asleep as if she had never been awake, as if some ghost, some angel had stolen into her body and possessed it, possessed me with it for a short time, finding exile from the wrath of winter, and then fled. Eleanor is like that sometimes—awake, possessed, then abandoned, then altogether different. Now she is asleep.

Three months later. Ninety days. She is dead. Gone. I am waking on a warmer morning in an icehouse. A northeaster is draining the cold from the Arctic and drenching the coast. On a May morning the house, the windows, the chimney are all glazed with ice and I am trapped within this brittle, perfect shell. The bed yawns out like a cavern beside me. I am afraid to move, afraid to believe again that she is not there. Fear strikes deep to the root of my being. It is impossible that I am alone and if I can skate along the perimeter of sleep, I can yet believe that she is still there. I can sense her weight on the springs, her softness wrapping around me always. I can almost keep from crying. I remain frozen like that for an hour. I can see the wind-up clock from here. It shows a bland, civilized, impersonal face to me and trickles time away with its childlike tapping. It belittles what I know and cares nothing of what I've lost. This cannot be possible for I believe that the world of inanimate objects is powerfully aware of the loss. A great savage arm has swept through here and torn the universe in half, a vandalized sail in the northeast blast of cold wind. I must focus on a task to stitch the world back together, however slipshod and temporary the work might be.

Two feet on the floor. Another impossible task completed. I'm willing to perpetuate the illusion. I get up, throw on work pants and an old flannel shirt that finds its way nightly to the backless chair by the window that we once called a stool. My feet find slippers, old worn-out leather things that remember the smell of instep, and I test my hand on the frame of the door. Some stupefying magic has held together the already shattered universe with mystifying glue for one more night. It is cold in here. The fire has gone out. This fact insists that I am still alive, that I get on with the immediacy of comfort. I remain forever thankful of that fact and wonder how anyone human can begin a day without the insistence that he bargain with the environment for a more optimum temperature.

The woodstove is cold. All the embers have turned to grey corpses. I move slowly but with such will and purpose that I can almost convince myself that I care. From the wood closet I take out the front pages of *The Mail Star* from over a year ago. Prince Charles and Diana had been smiling their way through the Maritimes, quipping with the press, thanking the gloating politicians, preening and shaking hands. It was such a perfect burlesque that Eleanor and I had toasted them with a bottle of Chipman's apple cider as we watched their ship, the Brittania, steam past our headland bound for the colonial outpost at Halifax Harbour. Eleanor and I had talked of empires won, but only I lived on to stake out the wasteland of empires lost. I light the match to the banner headline and toss bits of old wood shakes on the flame. Then more small wood, old fenceposts, and finally quartered logs, hardwood—maple from miles inland where trees are permitted the luxury of giving up life for a winter and reclaiming it in spring.

I have conquered the light of morning another time, defeated darkness and congratulated the terror of the spring-time onslaught of an Atlantic storm. The pride of heat pushes against my face until I am flushed and uncomfortable as I crank back the air supply and make room for the house to warm completely. In an hour or so, the glazing will slip off the windows and drip down the cedar shingles back into the soil. I'm headed for the kitchen and will fumble around in the refrigerator looking for the eggs, then fumble through a cupboard looking for tea. Then I will light the kitchen fire in the cookstove and make more cold steel turn warm and useful. Something inside would have me go racing out into the wind, the freezing rain and the sloppy snow, run deep into the unthawed forest of winter and stand perfectly still until I have become a grotesque ice statue.

But I won't. For now I have reason to continue to do what I am doing. I am, perhaps, satisfied again simply to be alive. These small things are enough.

————Muriel and the Baptist

Eleaner's wife

On the other side of Rocky Run there's a crooked finger of land that stretches into the sea. When the sky is low and grey and knifed clean by north winds I look over at those dark red palisades of Penchant Point and think of Muriel, alone with her God and three towers. You can almost see the narrow strait of open sky electric with invisible communications. Muriel of the open Gideon Bible, Muriel of the unshadowed kingdom, speaker in tongues, interpreter of dreams, enemy of the Voice of America.

Once a year she would travel the shore, and try to force truth into our souls, to save us from hell, to indoctrinate us with the law of a book. She could only ever half-read, but that was enough. Her eyes burned like hot coals and there was always fear and mistrust of anything in this world in the flames. In brief flashes you could see love, a love we knew nothing of, a love for a tyrant God, a Giant MacAskill of a being who shouted to her in the wind, instructing her to remind the world of the fire below. It burned beneath her house in a damp secret flame at night and no one could feel its heat quite like she could. Muriel was one of those women you could take a knife to and she wouldn't bleed. The flame had dried the blood in her veins and lit the torch in her eyes and, like so many believers in such power, she was more than capable of murder.

* * *

On a raw spring day, Muriel would show up just when I was finally set to paint the house and she wouldn't let me alone until she had preached the full gospel all pumped up with her own venom. She spit as she talked, not on purpose, but because the fire inside wanted to get rid of the dampness and let the flame rule. Eleanor and I would weather her storm and invite her in for tea once she was worn out, which took some doing. It was dangerous to invite her in if she had not worn herself down. Once she kicked the sleeping dog underneath the table so hard that she cracked his rib and we had to have it set. She apologized, knowing it wasn't her but the devil who had wrenched the spasm in her leg. The devil, she said, was often the messenger from God sent to let her know white by showing black clear as midnight. Eleanor would always say to me that Muriel was a kind woman, that it took a little to see beneath it all to the loneliness and softness that was barricaded up behind a skin like white bone itself. To me, she was like the lobster, the crab, or the sea urchin: she wore her skeleton on the outside. Eleanor insisted that we should be kind to her. And we were.

Muriel was maybe twenty years above me and a pioneer of sorts in that she preceded the rest of us who live our lives out alone on this coast of forgotten people, quiet strangers in a world of noisy crowds. Primitives left to live out what's left on the coastline of a forgotten fringe of a continent gone mad with machinery and power and empty promises. If I live forever as planned, I will confuse the new generation with my very knowledge of the world of sail, of tide, of wind and wood. They will see me as a museum and the public will pay good money to enter into me and become the past.

When Muriel's Baptist came to Penchant Point, we had never heard of Baptists in these parts. He wore work clothes and carried that book, the one she kept for her own. There was no bridge then and I was a kid, greasing oarlocks by the inlet, who offered him the ride across to Penchant. He spoke the whole way, never thanked me, but said the Lord was to be my anchor, this to a person who then believed in perpetual motion. I would let nothing tether me to a sunken weight but preferred to swim wild with any current handy. The Baptist wore shoes the size of anchors themselves and he had a curious pallor, a blondness in the skin with a blue-grey and soft tan just underneath. No doubt he was a mix of black and white. I wanted to know more about that, but he wanted to speak only of Guiding Lights and more so about punishment, not skin colour. His voice boomed as if it had been shaped out of rock and, each time he spoke, he was throwing a hewn boulder at the sky.

"How did you get here?" I asked him. He seemed to me like someone who had come from a place very far away.

"A man walks," he answered. "A good man walks upright." He had such a cold, sure sense of himself. I would like to have untied the knot that held his tongue back, so when we reached the other side, I stood rather stupidly shaking his hand and asked him how far he had come and from where.

"Today I walked here from North Preston. Before that I walked as a child under the hand of the Lord with my daddy from Virginia. We did some walking in those days. My daddy had walked back and forth in a dirt field working for a sinner, but before him his father walked free in Africa, a pagan who had never spoken the name of the Lord. We are different now." He said the word *we* like he was referring to all three of them. Staring into his face, I suddenly realized how much older he was than I first thought, and unlike any man I had seen on the shore before. The Baptist had steel girders for shoulders and poured concrete for a body so that when he stood up it was like he pushed the earth down beneath him from his force.

The Baptist wanted to know about the people out on Penchant Point and I told him his preaching might be better accepted elsewhere since the families of Penchant were hard, untrusting creatures, each tied down to farms of rock-strewn pasture and thin topsoil for generations. He smiled. "But I've come to speak to the people." So I offered to take him to the first house on the crooked little trail that stretched like a broken-backed snake to the ultimate narrow steep headland that barely held out against the corrosion into the sea.

Lincoln MacQuarrie was the unlikeliest of candidates for the Baptist's kingdom of God. We found him behind his barn in his turnip field trying to pry a rock from the ground with a ten-foot pole, a contrary ox with one bad leg, and more cursing than the Baptist had probably ever heard in his solemn life. Years later I would remember that rock when my first dentist, a man with stale alcoholic breath and a shaky hand, tried to pull out a tooth he claimed was rotten. "It's only holdin' by the nerve root," he told me and pulled until my jaw would have cracked, but still nothing ever came out. That rock was nerve-rooted deep into the planet with the devil at the other end of the nerve holding on for dear life. A man with an ox can move mountains but not with MacQuarrie's beast, who looked starved and starry-eyed and better suited for sleep than work.

"Dirty Jesus, would you look at this?" Lincoln asked the wind as I introduced the Baptist who held out his hand. MacQuarrie wouldn't take it, just kept wiping his bruised knuckles on a dirty handkerchief, his lower jaw quivering the way it always did like he was chewing air and turning it into something acid, his face all pinched up.

"Sir, I come in the name of Jesus," said the Baptist, towering over Lincoln, "Jesus who showed us the way. Be not aggrieved by your tribulations here below. But cast out the demon within and kneel before the Almighty!"

No doubt the Baptist meant well in his own heart but he was a trifle confused, having spent so much time walking, walking alone and making conversation only with the angels, for he appeared to lack the graces of idle shore talk in this land where men spoke at length on wind and tide and foul weather and the revenge of the North. MacQuarrie conceived that the

giant mulatto was some sort of crazy lunatic, who was asking
him to kneel before him as a heathen god. For the Baptist,
framed against the bleak, low-slung sky, sucked in his chest
and you could see muscles rippling like living serpents down
the length of his almighty neck. Many men before MacQuarrie
had confused the images of angel and devil, prophet and
satanist. And Lincoln had thought more than once that the
evil one would one day show his face and own up to the rotten
tricks he had so often personally afflicted on this peninsula.
So, Lincoln grabbed the pole and was about to make good his
revenge. There was nothing I could do but seek refuge behind
the ox and let philosophers contend.

The Baptist saw the pole raised above him but stood firm,
opened his Gideon, quoting slowly the words of Paul to the
Thessalonians: "We are bound to thank God always, for you
brethren, as it is meet, because your faith groweth exceed-
ingly and the charity of every one of you all toward each other
aboundeth."

The pole came earthward, and as if through a miracle or
some magic of his huge frame, the Baptist dropped low in a
wrestler's stance, bracing his hands above him in a mighty grip
to receive the message of the unbeliever. He caught the pole
and held firm while MacQuarrie chewed air and made good
the whites of his eyes. And as Lincoln stood frozen, a man with
irons locked to a circle of loose pebbles and goose tongue, the
Baptist lifted the weapon and advanced to the stone, drove it
hard beneath and executed a profound cantilever as the ox
moved forward of its own accord. The rock moved up, then
slipped back, then an unshaken Baptist heaved again, pulling
up the earth for a full foot outside the perimeter of the
unwanted inhabitant. With a shoulder, he pushed it aside and
you could see the thing lying there. Underneath, it had been
like an iceberg which fanned out in horizontal planes that had
kept it solid in the earth.

MacQuarrie had fallen flat on his back. He leaned up on an elbow from the weeds to see the vacant hole filling up with water from below. The Baptist hauled Lincoln to his feet, brushed off the farmer's shirt and turned to go.

Back on the road, the Baptist spoke in a slow, trembling voice, "The damned fools." I encouraged him that it might be easier from there on out but felt my own safety was not to be bargained with. I explained to the Baptist about the road, and its absurd crooked path. It passed through towns marked on an official map with names as if to believe that a town could be two houses less than a quarter-mile apart. Each town had been labelled with a binding, uncreative name—Upper Penchant, Middle Penchant, Lower East Penchant, Lower West Penchant and Lower Penchant itself.

The final house at the least habitable mile of the peninsula was where Muriel lived alone, with maybe twelve goats. I had been there once and seen a curious little hill, perfectly round and smooth like a bowl turned upside down, green as if it were a smooth-clipped cemetery and populated by goats and ravens, all perfectly placed so as to create some supreme balance and order. Two other hills, the same as the first but covered in stunted spruce and alders, followed and, beyond that, a phalanx of stone pointing to the sea. By the first green hill lived Muriel Cree, a large woman herself, a full six feet but bent at the neck and appearing as if she was always looking for something at her feet. I knew almost nothing of her then except that she was the daughter of a Portuguese sailor who had washed up here and taken for his wife a dark, brooding Penchant girl who had been out berry picking. Since the girl had always seemed odd, unexplainably dull-witted and prone to fits of madness and speeches in unaccountable animal languages, the family approved of the sailor. Muriel was their only child and she grew up alone with rocks and gulls and a few goats. Then when she was a teenager, her parents disappeared. It was said that a Portuguese ship drew in near shore

and the father flagged it down. The story suggests that they
simply embarked, leaving Muriel all alone at the end of the
earth to feed the goats, her with a bent neck and club foot.

I had turned back before reaching Lower East Penchant but
the Baptist found her at last, a woman with ears in the land of
the deaf. He thundered away as he had before until she was
convinced of his piety, then asked him to stay. The Baptist
stayed on after he had washed away her sins in a cold sea and
made her memorize all the names in the Old Testament. They
would chant them together in late December when winter
braced its feet against a cold northern rock and pushed hard
only to feel itself unready to convince a stalwart ocean. The
sea banked up its thick grey clouds to form swirling foothills
in the sky, holding onto what heat it had dared to absorb
through the warm months and not wanting to relent to the
icy pitchfork tongue of the Arctic.

The few rugged fishermen left who slid their boats past
Penchant heard the rattle of ancient names coming from
shore: "Obadiah, Malachi, Manaseh, Ephraim, Abraham,
Jacob, Isaiah, Zebulun, Helon, Milcah, Noah!"

It would not be for me to pretend an accurate reconstruction
of what sort of passions went into their name-shouting or what
it meant. I had heard, though, that the Baptist had stayed, that
he had married her in his own way, with himself as the
minister, with God his witness. With a vision of beginning a
new line of Israel, repopulating the Shore with a crowd of
Christians carrying the names of Deuteronomy and literate in
their hearts with the teaching of Jesus. It would have been a
curious mix with the pagans on this coast.

Toward his end, the Baptist found himself one morning
walking a ground of clean white frost that had sculpted blades
of grass into a valley of scimitars. He walked to the top of the
first hill leading the youngest of the tribe of goats that had
populated that point for seven of their generations. It was a
goat with a long white coat and one long mark across its neck
like a black scar. To the Baptist it seemed like an instruction
from the Almighty to cut along the line, to offer up sacrifice

*common
God*

for his bloodthirsty God who had found satisfaction in seeing blood, even the blood of His own Son, seep into the earth for renewal and rebirth.

The goat had two marbles for eyes and, at the center of each, a green diamond displaced from a night star. They were unblinking eyes that might have been borrowed from a god or a devil for the Baptist had seen the goat stand upright in the wind on a November night beneath a full moon. Muriel had seen it too and without explanation she had taken a box of salt out and sprinkled it in a circle on the grass. In the morning she found a perfectly circular formation where the green grass had been ripped out and the few inches of soil dug back so that nothing showed but a smooth, circle of seamless bedrock that had been polished clean as if someone had licked the stone to a shine.

For the Baptist, the sacrifice of the goat would help ensure that the human race would begin new and fresh in the new year. The goat did not blink as he held out the gutting knife and sliced along the line, watching its own blood fall on the green frost-white grass and then, in a matter of minutes, begin to freeze in a widening dark pond around itself and the Baptist. With virtually no struggle at all, it was like the creature had no qualms of giving up any rights it had on this earth. But when the last cup fell from the neck and splashed on the Baptist's shoes, the man found he could not move; his feet were frozen fast into the red ice and he looked up to see his wife standing there, her head bent over as she stared at the blood and let out a mournful wail. As she walked back to the house the Baptist had to take the knife and chip away at his shoes, without success. He removed his feet, leaving the shoes frozen stiff and stained red, then continued with his ritual, cutting alders and piling them in an arc toward the heavens, and then lifted the blood-drained carcass to the top.

With kerosene he doused the pile and attempted to send his offering above, but a cold, hard rain started, freezing instantly anything in its path. The pile glazed over in a matter of minutes and the tomb was ice, not fire, and remained like that

half the winter as the ice grew thicker but unclouded, staying
perfectly clear and building up so that it acted as a magnifying
lens, enlarging and distorting the impaired covenant. Had
anyone found his way this far out to the point in January he
would have seen one gigantic green diamond eye fixed on the
door of Muriel's house.

On that morning when the Baptist had found his way back
to the house, he was himself partially glazed and his bare feet
seemed to sweat blood. Muriel washed them in warm soapy
water then made a breakfast of oatcakes and saltfish.

On the third day of the ice storm, Muriel asked the Baptist
to go with her to the basement and pray there upon the
bedrock with bared knees and he did, shouting in his solemn
voice to the massive timbers that held up the floors above him,
speaking in tongues Biblical and unknown, but fearing for
once that the words might have come from Satan rather than
the Almighty, both having shared the same language once.

I relate this all to you as best I can by piecing together the
fragments of Muriel's own story from her numerous visits.
What happened next remains shrouded but Muriel took the
gutting knife to the Baptist, that is fairly certain, and she may
have watched his blood slide along the rock floor and settle
in tiny pools and maybe she left him there for the rats to gnaw
or perhaps she did something else. I'm not one to speculate
on that. But when she went back up into the warm house, she
had made her own offering to the Old Testament God and
consummated a difficult marriage beyond heaven's gates.

"personaly addressed narrative "you"

* * *

I was one of the few to have even met the Baptist and never
once considered his absence until the following year when
Muriel had begun her own preaching along Penchant, con-
demning the MacQuarries to a burning pit and requesting in
public the Lord to swallow up the men as they stood on the
wharf. But to me, she said only kind things and simply asked
me to read a bit of Revelations to her out loud, which I did in

my most proper schoolboy voice. For that she was grateful and annually, wherever I lived, she would seek me out and ask me to read.

The loss of the Baptist was unquestioned, but so were a great many other things along here and what we always said in public was this: "Probably fell off a boat and drowned," which was the way that so many went that it was said in much the same way that someone might have said that your neighbour was suffering from a cold, too bad. The goats increased and wandered all over the peninsula looking for better feeding ground. Many turned wild and found their way into the fields as far away as MacQuarrie's and, for years, you couldn't head over to that end of the land without somebody or other saying to watch out for the wild goats. At least one hunter had been reported to have been gored by the curled horns of a snow-white goat with a long shaggy coat, but everyone said it served him right because he was an American come up from the Boston States looking for moose and we didn't need his kind anyway. But the kids were warned off and generally no one really wanted to trust a car on that winding stretch of ruined earth called a road to see how Muriel was faring with her farm. Not until the Voice of America, the radio people who wanted to send messages to Europe, decided that the three low hills out near the tip of Penchant were just perfect for their radio towers. They inquired of the government the land's owner and found, to their delight, that Muriel didn't officially own any of her land anyway. And, oh, they were polite about it and said she could keep her house and her little kitchen garden and the barn but that the three gentle hills of such perfect geometry must go to the Voice and so they did.

Some of the construction crew shot a few of her goats and she tried to set fire to a bulldozer, but the RCMP came for the first time ever and said she would have to go if she didn't co-operate. So she went back to shouting names from the Old Testament at the sea as the radio people skewered the sky with three giant towers, each with evil blinking red lights, each sending invisible messages in foreign tongues to people on another continent.

Muriel realized that she may well have sinned in the eyes of the Almighty back there in the time of the Baptist and knew that the sinister blazing red light of the tower had a message for her too. The Lord did move in mysterious ways and had taken his time with settling up accounts with her. And she was grateful for that.

Many years after the towers were built, she would visit us and explain how she prayed daily on her bare knees in her basement on a certain circumference of smoothed bedrock, that, she said, she kept polished with her own tongue. She had shown Eleanor and me her knees which looked misshapen and gnarled like old cat spruce limbs. The skin had a tough, leathery callus like the hide of some animal. She would ask if we would allow her to kneel for a while and pray on our own floorboards and we would always oblige her. Afterwards she would thank us and compliment the softness of our boards. Then she would ask for a cup of tea and we would sit quietly together like we were all the most civilized, gentle people on the face of the earth.

Losing Ground

When I was thirteen, my best friend was John Kincaid. In late spring the lifeblood of the planet began to run free and the gaspereau were making their way up inside the land. John was a hard knot of a kid with chipped bones from falling off back steps and close-cropped hair over a skull that suited the Reaper himself. He was always unhappy, dissatisfied with everything, primed with so much anger it shot out his arm like electricity. He threw things—rocks, wood, fists—because his father had hit him so often, pounded fear and hate into him in the evenings so that he would come out into the world and throw it around at everything. He always wanted to teach me how to kill things and I hated him for that, for his private unbent cosmology of crippling living things and siding with the blatant burning deathwish of all things that moved. But there was a kind of love between us although I could never have called it that. The emotional economics of our ageing had dismantled what little love we had and sent it off to scrap yards where we would have to go looking one day for the rusted remains so that we might rehabilitate the engines of childhood and translate love into sex and sex into love and believe again in girls and women. It would not be impossible, but for now the corrosion was effective and we were all but lost.

So John Kincaid and I were by the brook where it swept soft curves of cold water light up into the sky and sped unsalted freshness into the sea forever. This tiny stream went miles inland to find its source at a stagnant, weed-choked pond that grew mosquitoes in summer and hatched dragonflies the size of toy airplanes and spawned frogs free and restless for Kincaid killings. But here at the edge of salt, the last instant of fresh water about to salt down its blood for good, we sat on a rare sunlit afternoon waiting for gaspereau to come flapping up the shallow brook so that we could do what? Catch them to eat? We had tried that once. "Better to eat razors," John had said. "Better to sit down to a plate of hot sewing needles and chew hard, better to swallow fried radio tubes and wire." The gaspereau were hopeless fish to us. Somebody's mother (it was reported at school) cooked the fish for three days straight until all the bones were dissolved and a cord of softwood consumed and then you could sit down to a plateful of mush which almost still tasted of fish while you could be assured your house would stink of gaspereau until Christmas. No, I don't think we had hope of catching them to eat.

I didn't even care to catch one. It was too easy, too pointless. To Kincaid, it was as if they hovered offshore all winter waiting for a chance to slap themselves out of the deep into the thinning waters of an unnamed brook looking for his stones to club them to death. Each year I hoped Kincaid would be different, that the death lunatic in him would die out so that he could go on with life, but I always expected too much of him.

Then they appeared. I always felt my own blood race to my head to see a still and shining surface go mad with an avalanche of life, a vast churning orgasm of fish splashing about in a fevered dance to snake themselves up the stream, to swim between rocks and trade up salt for fresh. They were there on this late afternoon in May. It was so beautiful that I almost forgot to see the damn boulder that blasted John was holding over his head ready to go, ready to get in the first bash at the first flawed creature who found his way inside the rock's shadow. But as I turned and saw him ready to pound I decided this was the year he had to change.

So I tackled him and the rock came down hard on my back as we poured down into the wet moss. He let go a flock of curses, learned from a professional, his father, a man with the devil's own dictionary under his skull. I could feel the weight of the pain drive down my spine from John's ancient weapon but I didn't care. He tried to grab a dead branch to skewer me and, had I not known him, I would have run for my life, figuring he would kill me instead of fish, death having its warrant out and willing to settle for spilled blood, cold or hot. But I kept him busy. I knew his spirit and knew he could fight, but so could I for different reasons. We were so equally powered that there could never be a winner. John had an easy temper to strike but his hate could only drive him so far. I simply had a stupid sort of stubbornness that wanted me to finish whatever I started. So we both fought till we bled enough to satisfy our pride. Then we quit. The fish were gone, the first wave of the year safely upstream in deeper pools for the coming night. And Kincaid didn't care then. A fight was as good as a bucket of bloodied fish and we were friends as usual. John said he'd kill me next time and I said, "Try."

Later that spring a man from Halifax came out with a pickup truck and a pair of pitchforks. Kincaid and I were walking up the road to the railroad bridge and this guy pulled over and asked us if we wanted to make a few cents shovelling fish. We both said, sure, and got in the truck where we had to sit on bare springs that had torn free of the seat. The radio was on, but there was nothing but static. Mr. Otto Bollivar, the man said his name was, and that we could call him Mr. Bo-liver but we didn't call him anything. And then he asked where he could find a good gaspereau run and I knew enough to shut up.

But John spoke up sharp, ready to give out time-honoured secrets that sent us straight to the spot. Mr. Bollivar was pleased and started coughing like maybe he would die or something if he didn't quick light a cigarette that he had to roll first. That seemed to stop the coughing. He threw me a pitchfork that would have gone through my boot if I hadn't moved quick. He told John, "Here. Use this net, it'll do."

"I ain't helping you with the fish," I said. Mr. Bo-liver looked at me like I said I was born on Jupiter.

"I'm paying you, ain't I?" He hadn't said how much.

"How much?" John wanted to know.

"Twenty cents a piece. Now shut up and let's get to work." I could already see that the stream was wrestling with itself the way that it does when the gaspereau are running.

"Look, you can't eat the damn things anyway," I shouted at him. He was a townie, a stupid city-slicker who probably didn't know. Instead of thanking me for saving him the work, he dropped his pitchfork, bit down on his cigarette and angled over to me.

"You know that. And I know that. But them stupid buggers in Halifax don't know cod tongue from coffin hinges. They'll buy it if it's the right price. And it'll be the right price." He coughed up something and spit a wad of yellow, awful phlegm on the ground.

"Forget it," I told him, "twenty cents or no twenty cents," and I walked on home. I knew Kincaid would stay and he did. Later, he told me that he got the full forty cents which was a lie because he only got a dime, if he got that.

* * *

A couple of years after that, John Kincaid and I had our own boat. It was a boy's boat because no man would ever have set foot in it, at least not in the condition that it was in. It wasn't what you call a skiff and it wasn't a dory and, as far as we could figure, it wasn't anything that anybody had a fixed name for.

We found her right side up in the wide marsh at the foot of Rigger's Lake in the winter. When the lake froze over, you could go walking out there and feel the arctic winds bear down until it made you feel good, all cold and clean inside like someone had just taken lye powder to your soul and you wanted to just suck in that cold frozen air, let it paralyze your nose hairs, then knife down into your chest. It felt that good. Kincaid and I didn't have ice skates but we liked to slide our feet out across the glazed wilderness. No one ever felt as free as we did then and it didn't catch up to us until the north wind drove white teeth marks into us with frost bite. Then we'd have to run back home and sit in front of the cookstove where our faces bloomed beet-juice red and our legs, Lord how they'd itch, but we knew for sure we were alive.

I think it was hunters who had lost the boat, or simply left the damn thing. It was half-rotten, poorly made to begin with, and filled with brown tide frozen up to the oar locks. Ironically, it was me who was the first to pick up a rock and want to bash in the sides just for the hell of it. But Kincaid, God, the light of Jesus took over his eyes because he had before him a *boat* and a rotten, dull and worthless thing, but a boat, a miracle, a frozen revelation from on high, the possibilities of life-ever-after and the means he had been looking for. He stopped my hand and let the rock fall at our feet, sending out a giant crack in the ice that shot northward halfway to Truro. "We've found a frigging boat," was all he said. Water seeped up from the crack and I worried that we had split the whole bloody planet in two, that it would turn inside out and the devil would present himself out of the depths and thank us for setting him free for good. He would have ice for a beard and icicles for hair and white blinding stones for eyes, for we knew that the Bible had gone through a number of translations and was all wrong. Hell was a cold, frozen place, damp and bone-numbing like a winter fog.

But nothing happened, save the setting free of one devilish spirit. The boat. I had never seen John so dedicated and so gentle. First we used dead limbs cracked off of marsh spruce, then we tried chipping away the ice like Indians with sharp stones and finally Kincaid ran off all the way to Baylor McNulty's chopping block to confiscate Baylor's double bit

axe for the rescue, while I stood guard as if there were hordes
of other half-wits out wandering the frigid waste land wanting
to salvage the carcass of this pathetically contrived duck hunting boat, fragile as an egg shell and rotten as the politics in
Halifax.

But Kincaid made good with the axe and chipped away like
a sculptor until it was free and all the worse for it. Then he let
out a long, maniac yelp in triumph. "We got our boat, Joney
boy," he repeated three times over and I knew what it meant
to him and I wanted it to mean as much to me. I knew it would
always be Kincaid's but we'd have to do it together, whatever
was to be done with that ice devil. So we dragged it home
across two miles of frozen grass and paper-ice shelving left
high and dry by a retreating tide. The blasted thing was heavy
as lead over the rough little hillocks of chumped-up ice that
had corrugated in the shallows. She was still weighted down
with the freight of her own brown ice and Kincaid wouldn't
let me touch the inside, fearing I'd split the gunwale and
destroy whatever mysterious vortex of spiritual energy held
the boat together. There we were, human flesh hauling dead,
brown frozen water two miles over a pitiless lake in a gale come
down special delivery from Hudson Bay. So of course we made
it. All the way to Kincaid's back step and sure he wanted to
haul the thing inside to thaw, only we would have had to
remove the door frame, then chase out his father, propped
up like a mannequin with a bottle in the kitchen listening to
a near-shot radio playing opera.

You have to understand that John's father had lost the boat
he owned to the bank and the government, he wasn't sure
which, but the boat was gone. Not a boat like ours but a real
Cape Islander with a German engine of some kind and a
couple of sails. It was just about the biggest boat that anybody
had seen on this shore for one man to own and to fish with
and you wanted to see that pile of cod it would deliver. Only,
something was frigged with the way the world worked because
one day the people wanted to eat cod, the next day, so the
buyer said, you couldn't give it away with pitchforks for a

penny and what do you do with a boat with an engine yet and a hungry bank and a government that has made promises for you? Inevitably, the boat was lost, sent to Halifax, and set up in drydock where it would rot until the economy improved or until folks got their taste buds back for cod or mackerel but none too soon at that.

George Kincaid galvanized himself with illegal rum and swore to God Almighty that he should have become a runner of rums himself like his father had suggested and used that German engine for some good business and let the fish go to hell. But he had been stupid. Here he already owed Lance Inkpen more money for his booze, what with nothing coming in. And what could you do but sit around in your own venom and get good and angry at everybody and nobody and forget about ever being the man you once were? John's mother had become a ghost. She was there but she wasn't. She always made the meals and then it was like she slipped into a trance and waited for George to cancel himself out for the day. Late at night, John said, she waltzed around the kitchen alone with the radio on and hummed. This didn't make a damn bit of sense to him. He thought she was cracked. But he believed in his old man.

John couldn't wait for spring to loose the chains on the boat of his, so he set to carving out the ice with a hand axe ever so slow and painstakingly and once I tempted him to pour hot water on her, but he shot the idea down, fearing it would crack the molded ribs and the boat itself would melt into the soil. Maybe it would just drain away in the spring rain or simply self-destruct, evaporate or dissolve.

Finally, a tense winter sun in late February began to burn holes through the snow piled on the roof and Johnny hauled out some old framed windows to set over the boat. By the end of the afternoon, she was dry and sound. Sound and solid as cork. You could have put your fingernail through her just about anywhere but this didn't bother John at all and, what the hell, I was getting excited. "She'll take a little paint. That's all she needs," I said for no good reason. Good God, then I

Vulnerability in a tough emotional landscape

had to turn away, because John Kincaid was about to cry and for once I realized I loved him. I didn't know up until that time that you could love a friend. But I let it be at that. I couldn't say a word, knowing that it was the same sort of love John felt toward me for saying something so foolish in his favour and believing that this pitiful gathering of planed spruce was more than a memory gone sour.

* * *

Sopping spring again. Cold, damp and angry with life there just beneath the surface ready to break the locks and sweat itself into summer. The ground cracked finally one day and was about to swallow up the cars and the horses and pull man back to mud at last. The boat had been glazed to lightning gloss with stolen green paint so that when the sun broke like warm champagne on our navy she sang bright chords of sea shanties locked up in her rotten wood. We had to carry her half a mile to Rigger's Lake, then farther down the shore to where the ice had given up and salt water lapped fresh. The gulls still sat on the ice in favour of winter and they watched as we slid our hopes out into the blue-green water. Kincaid was in a trance, a spiritual ecstasy, a man of water at last. To hell with land, such a sad substitute for the floating world. A man arrived, a child acquitted, a soul saved.

"Sit down, before we both drown," I told him as he danced about lightly as a sandpiper and crazy to boot. He sat. We were floating, oarless, the obvious tools forgotten, left on the shores. What did we know of reason? Left to himself, John would have let the current slip him out to sea as soon as it was able. He didn't care. I did.

"Dig, damn it!" I chastised him, meaning to use his hands. We had to quick paddle back to shore, retrieve the ends to our means. It was like pulling Lucifer out of heaven. But I made the lunatic dig.

Each leaning over a side, we plied the water up to our elbows, in slow painful strokes. God Himself had performed a dirty miracle and allowed this body of water to stay liquid well below the freezing point. It was like dipping your arms full-length

winter surfer
9

into a barrel of razor blades and stirring them up. The cold was magnificent, absolute and horrendous. John howled from the pain. My arm cramped up and I had to switch. It was maddening and wonderful. The logic of boats, of currents, was not with us and we lost ground, only to be saved by a sunken trunk that nabbed the boat just as we were about to slip into the channel itself and make ready for the sea where the waves were cracking like fireworks over the rocks at the shallow mouth of Rocky Run. I jumped for shore and landed on a wafer-thin shelf of ice left from another tide, then danced through sheets of glass and jeweller's mud until I was on the bank with the rope.

"Good work, Joney, good work," Kincaid rattled, not shaken a bit. Death and life were all the same to him now he had the boat. Either way he was saved.

* * *

In the summer that followed the salvation of the boat, we were at it. Fishing. Making real money. Not much, but our own. Cod, hake, haddock, mackerel. Sold to women for half its worth and only the best fish. Independence. John, a changed creature. Self-respect, pride, the ability to stand the world forever. In August the sun turned benevolent and peeled our shirts off, then painted our skin red. Even the water warmed against its better judgement. By our own tiny wharf, we gutted and scraped and heaved heads to gulls and pretended it would go on like this forever—blue sky, mica-mirrored fish scales electric with light; it was like some wonderful balloon was bursting in my chest. There was nothing to do but wait till Kincaid had put down his knife for an instant to wipe snot and I launched at him and we arced off the wharf through a cloud of herring gulls and into the inlet, slapping down on the afternoon chop like tandem divers. Ten feet of water, hardly more. Green-blue, with seaweed at the bottom and crabs in miniature armies shuttling away from the invasion.

The miracle of ignorance is always a wonder to behold. John's ignorance in not being able to swim a stroke and my own at never once realizing the obvious fact. Kincaid held on around my throat with a wrestling hold and tried to pull me down to where it seemed he wanted to writhe upon the rocky bottom. I understood his curses even below air and feared for us both. I had often noticed my inability to remain civilized when deprived of oxygen and John obviously shared that affliction. Kicking him in the gut to free the elbow bent around my Adam's apple, I pushed away and shot up for air, only to be hauled back down by a lead anchor around my feet. John, somehow refusing to even flap his way up to kiss air, preferred death for us all, but a man without legs is not without arms to whip about and fight for lung privileges. So I too cursed and hauled and hoped that, in fact, Kincaid held on, which he did, knowing nothing else below the waterline but my socks and the kick of my shoes in his face. And even after I had regained shore, it was like he didn't want to give up in the shallows till I crawled up across the stones and busted glass, at least one of us still human. John finally heaved himself up on a stump and coughed and vomited and let go of the blue in his skin. It wasn't a pretty picture.

"You can't swim, you bastard," I swiped.

"In a boat you don't need to swim."

"In our boat you do. You could kill us both."

"Seemed like you were the one out for killing."

"The hell I was. Look, you stupid fisherman, if you want to fish, you bloody well better learn to swim."

"My father don't swim and neither does any man on this shore who fishes."

"Stupid, God Almighty. I'll teach you to swim."

"Never in a million years."

I didn't have that much time, but I knew damn well Kincaid was going to do nothing but fish for the rest of his days and if he couldn't swim, he might be getting a sad discount on his career.

"I'm not going back in that damn boat with you until you can tread water."

"Go to hell with you."

I left fifty pounds of fresh cod on the cutting table to rot and walked home.

I stewed over it for three weeks until the first hurricane cut loose from Barbados and made unwholesome threats outside my windows on an evil, dark night. I wondered how many days John would wait for the swell to die off before he would try to run the inlet. He seemed to have no fear of waves and was masterful at rowing our frail little craft right out through ten-foot breakers, then on our way home, skate us down the face of a wave nearly into the railroad bridge. I couldn't let him continue alone. Besides, I missed the boat myself so I joined him the next day and we tempted eternity once on the way out and once on the way in with a haul of fish that should have sunk a boat twice our size. John was cocky and corrupted by his victory, his ability to cheat fate and the fact that I had given in.

Only I hadn't. I waited until the first of November, knowing that we'd have to quit soon anyway. The water temperature was still less than cauterizing. On a dead calm sea, just beyond the shallows of the run, I waited for John to start untangling a hand line, then quickly hauled the hand axe out of my pack and, with a single swift blow, chopped a hole through the bottom of the boat that sent the axe diving toward a mussel bed. It was only a matter of seconds before the boat was swamped and I made a dive for it over the side, away from my panicked partner.

Maybe some boats don't sink, but ours was not one of them. The sea was greedy and I knew soon it would want Kincaid but it wouldn't be today. I let him curse and let him flounder and stayed close enough so he would fight hell itself to get his hands around my neck but good God, he swam. He swam like a dragon breathing fire, a runaway water-wheel, a venomous roiling inhuman thing, but he swam.

We landed ashore on fresh clean sand, white and fine as snow, Kincaid out of breath and boiling in the blood. He thought I had gone mad but wanted to kill me before I had a chance for a cure. He found a rock the size of a marker buoy and charged at me, wanting my skull. I was ready and moved off, waited for him to change weapons and come at me with fists. I let him plant two angry jabs in my face before I made my exit, knowing I had done good and realizing we could never be friends again.

The boat was not to be saved. But Kincaid had enough money laid by to put a payment down on a larger vessel, something close to a real fishing boat. He set out to double, then triple our old catch while I went back to school where I learned to recite Shakespeare's sonnets and read books by other dead Englishmen until I dreamed them in my sleep. John Kincaid didn't speak a word to me for over fifty years.

And then the year came for all things to die, the year for me to rant against death, to establish eternity once and for all and to quiet forever all losses. November. The months are very important to me. Name a month and it rings inside me like a sound, a colour, a package of emotion and smell. Eleanor gone. November, pulling out the rocks from beneath the foundation of the hill, waves catapulting up the sheer dirt cliff and spiralling pirouettes of spray around to boil with the wind on a wild, grey night. Kincaid, finally dead. The news on the radio. Not one, but three boats from the harbour out at sea in late afternoon on a senseless, stupid ocean, blinded by instinct. Kincaid himself, refusing as usual to give it up, the tides good and high, the catch thick and heavy, no more debts to pay on any man's boat or mortgage and his greed thick and running full-steam for a man my own age. Sixty-nine. Sixty-eight actually. The reporter on the radio said he was sixty-eight. All those years. I could never have believed him to be younger than me. Kincaid. He never really spoke to me again since the hatchet work. He had walked the shore waiting for the boat but found only splinters with the right paint. The hand axe, by some uncommon, messianic whim of the sea, had made its way to the beach and John Kincaid found it, planted it in the side of our house like any Indian.

It would have been the right night for John to die. A monster sea, the highest of tides and him a couple of miles out from here, tangled in kelp, a chance for the catch to get back at him. And my bloody trick had probably done nothing more than increase the agony, make it harder to die which is to say give death more power. How many other blunders had I done in my life? How often had a well-meaning gesture caused a sufferer more pain?

I switched off the radio and calmed the kettle on the wood stove, then sat in dark silence staring again at completion. The tidiness of it all. Too simple, too easy. And I could at that moment fall on the floor and writhe if I wanted, alone on a sea cliff with my private hell. The loss. Eleanor, then John. The desire so great to wail, to pound my head against a wall or do myself in, to complete it once and for all. Yet I could also do quite the opposite now. And did. I could set it all outside of me and look it dead in the dark face and not be mad and not be terror-struck and not be unhappy at all. And I turned on a light and made room in the warm kitchen for us all.

It was then that John Kincaid ripped open the door and barged in wanting blood.

"I could swim, you bastard. Look at me, MacPherson. The man saved. Twice saved is twice too many."

"Get over here by the fire, John. You're alive, I don't believe it. Thank God."

Instead of thanking God, he tried to kill me. It was perhaps the third time in my life he fully tried to do it. We were both old men now but it was the same. He grabbed a piece of split hardwood and tried to bash my brains out and I shielded myself only enough to feel the blunt weapon connect on bone but no meaty grey matter. I let him try to do what he had decided upon, but he was weak and his own violence finally sent him flat to the floor where he bunched up a rug and sobbed into its dust.

He had been in the sea two full hours, pounded by thirty-foot waves and groping from one stick of salvage to another. He had heaved his guts into the cold sea three times, and gone unconscious twice only to come around for the last time with water invading his lungs and no feeling in his feet and fingers but his arms continuing to flap on their own as they moved like machines, long after he had wanted them to quit, long after he had schemed a will to drown himself, to end the stupid fight. He would have been happy. But instead he swam, his body worked the waves, not him. And then he felt a hand, something like a fist, pull him up into the air, then smash him down into the terrifying mass of white foam, a shuddering torment of water that twisted him around and around until he couldn't tell up from down. His skull was nearly wrenched from his neck and his eyes were stuck wide open. "I've seen hell, thank you. And it's white and it's grey and it moves like cold snakes around your throat and makes you scream inside your head."

The grey and white hell had tried to break his back three times, lifting him and dropping him on the rocky stubble at the base of my hill until his dead fingers reached and found red mud. Then he knew he was alive and wanted to be dead.

Kincaid drank tea and then he drank rum. He refused a trip to the hospital and for that he later lost the tips of three fingers and two toes. In the morning he cried for over an hour and I had to leave the house, hovering nearby for fear he'd slice his wrists but he didn't. Nor did he go to sea again. He took the insurance money and holed up with a cranky bitch of a woman who kept three other old men. He was obliged to turn over to her all of his savings and there he sat, before a television with the smell of stale urine forever in the air. When I would go to visit him, he would say my name but that was all.

_____The War Comes Home

The world wars baffled me and made me feel different from the rest. I couldn't conceive of the great battles being fought on foreign soil and the barbarism of enemies or the meaning of three-inch newspaper headlines. I had been carving my own private economy out of fish guts and pulp wood and, while I suspected it wasn't enough to make a life from, I knew where I was and what I was doing. But then I woke up one morning and all the men were gone except for me and the old farts who piss off the wharf. It was like the sun didn't seem to come up in the same spot anymore.

It took one world war to blast me out of Halifax and kill my mother and a second one to pull me back into that city. I walked all the way back to that city and felt different with every step that took me toward the alien world and away from my own private coastline with the handful of people I knew to be my own. The ferry was filled with uniforms and smelled of cigarettes and oil. I asked one of the uniforms what I had to do to get into the war and he gave me the once-over like I spoke a strange enemy language. He had a thin face that looked like it had been chipped out of flint. You know the way

that flint only breaks off at just a certain angle then leaves
depressions; it was like that. A cigarette was glued to his upper
lip and pointed toward the deck, held there by some sort of
magic and trailing one blue line of smoke up into his eyes so
that he squinted in a way that you knew he liked considerably.

"The war ain't on this side, bud," he said to me in a condes-
cending way, even though I knew he was a good deal younger
than me. But he was bolstered up by that uniform and saw *MacLennan*
himself as something slightly larger than life. He told me
about an office on Hollis Street where I should go, so I headed
straight for it as soon as the ferry bumped into the pilings.
Only a few blocks away I found the tall soot-blackened building with a queue of ragged men waiting in line outside.
Standing behind the last man in place I felt like I was in a soup
line, a refugee from my own country not so many miles away
but existing somehow on a different plane of existence
altogether. So little of what I had read in the papers had
seemed real to me and now I could see why. I felt like some
misplaced phantom that had shown up here on the concrete
sidewalk in Halifax among a rabble of men who looked like
they had slept the night in doorways.

I asked the man in front of me if this was the right place.

"Right, if you're looking for a ticket to get yourself killed,"
he said. He half-turned to say the words but stood looking at
the wall instead of me. Although he couldn't have been as old
as forty, he spoke with a voice borrowed from the bottom of a
mine and there was a mucousy film over one of his eyes.

"I'm looking forward to the food," he told me. "They give
you plenty to eat before they get you killed."

I think that if it hadn't been for the radio, I might not have
been here, a phantom on a cold, dismal street. I would have
stayed put. I had always had faith in the powers of good and
evil creating their own balance in the world. One could never
really get the final hold on the other, so it seemed futile to
have to go off and fight an empire gone mad. Then the news
came to me through a government letter that my father,
himself a phantom now for many years, had been serving on

a civilian supply ship, carrying food to England from Canada. A torpedo had sunk her somewhere off the coast of Ireland. All but twelve had found their way back to civilization but observers had sworn that all had arrived safely ashore. It seemed he had simply disappeared in Ireland up around Donegal Bay and that was all there was to be said. Since he hadn't actually been in the military, it wasn't desertion. Maybe he just found some people he liked and wanted no more of sinking ships.

"Nothing left to enlist but old men with empty skulls like us," the shabby hulk in front of me said, trying to be polite. *Old* was a funny way of putting it. But maybe thirty-three was old. No teenagers here. They were already gone, shot up on a bloodied ridge in France or waiting to splash ashore against the enemy this very minute. If I had been the last man in line, I would have left, gone to find some black coffee and dirty spoon in a Hollis Street coffee shop. But now there were at least ten men behind me, all as unkempt as the man in front of me. A door up ahead opened and everyone in line up to me was allowed in. I was the last of the batch. A dark hallway, then a long flight of stairs and a butch-faced woman handing out forms to be filled. Men laughing. I didn't get it. Fumbling with pencils, coughing, spitting, admission one by one that the language of paper was not anything they were familiar with. I filled mine out and handed it back to the clerk promptly. She frowned, as if I had committed an offense, not taken it seriously enough, or fudged the answers. By tilting her head to the side, I was to understand that she wanted me to go into the next room.

A door shut behind me and I was face to face with a mushroom-shaped man in a white coat sitting on a stool. His face was bloated and rubbery and he smoked a cigarette through a black holder. "Close the door please," he said. As I did so, he opened a bottle of pills and gulped down about five. "Painkillers. Everybody wants to kill something. I just like to murder pain."

I didn't really understand what he was talking about.

"Don't mind me. Just a little morphine. I have to endure a
lot. Take off your shirt. And pants." He fumbled with the
stethoscope, coughed loudly and flicked ashes on the green
linoleum floor. "You're not one of the regulars. Come in from
the sticks?"

"Eastern Shore, if that's the sticks?"

"Ever been to Larry's River?"

"Once." I remembered a barren hill of rock outcropping, a
church larger than all the houses of the village combined. A
brazen graveyard on the top of the hill with a gaudy painted
crucifix.

"I grew up there. Lived there until I was twenty-five. Kids
aren't allowed to grow up anymore. How come you waited so
late to enlist? You must be thirty yourself."

"Thirty-three. I don't know why."

"Those other guys out there. They ain't soldiers. Shoot their
foot off first time you give 'em a gun. They come because it
gives them something to do, makes them feel important. You
can't scrape up scum off a Halifax street and fight Hitler with
it. I'll go through the motions, then they get a cup of tea and
a few biscuits. We say we'll let 'em know. They were probably
all good men. Once." He opened his bottle of pills again and
popped a handful. He did look like he was in pain. Behind all
that weary flesh there was something fatherly about him. He
had a vulgar sort of charm, a sense of caring even as he talked
tough. The doctor leaned over as far as his bulk would permit
him and held the icy disc of the stethoscope up to my chest.
After listening for less than ten seconds, he leaned back.
"Damn. You're no good."

"What?"

"You're no soldier. Forget it. Something wrong with your
bloody heart."

"The hell?"

"Listen. You'll live. I give you maybe forty more years, fifty if
you eat right. You ain't fightin'."

"Why?"

"*Why?* Cause I said so. Go get married. Have a few kids. Somebody gotta raise the next generation." He was folding up the stethoscope and stood up, turning a broad, sloping white back to me. "I got a quota, but I'm gonna surprise one of the regulars. Send him up. Maybe they'll make him a general or something. You go get a job, lots of 'em around for a man who can stand straight." He saw a pained look on my face. I wanted a name for the terminal illness I had.

"Jesus, son. What's it *called?* It's called living. You start dying from the day you get spanked. It just takes some people longer than others to get around to it. I'd like it to take you a long time. Go back home. Live forever, see if I care." He looked out a window toward the harbour where military ships were steaming through the Narrows and, in a matter of minutes, would be beyond land, knifing waves toward Europe with men to spill blood, to save lives, to win back land. It started to snow a wet, pathetic slop. "C'mon. Get out. I'll file your form. Can't let them take a man in your condition." He winked.

A back door was opened and I was ushered out into another stairway painted in a foul, shiny green. The sound of my feet hitting the metal grates as I descended was unlike anything I had ever heard, a hollow sound like water dripping in a huge well. I was looking for the bottom of that well and waiting to be swallowed up in cold green water. Instead my hand found a door and I was looking out at the harbour.

* * *

There was no clear reason to me as to why people lived in cities. The life of one family vertical against the next, strangers huddled together behind a pile of bricks, each with a wall to call his own, a hotplate, a cramped bed. In a place like Nova Scotia, you grow up with elbows that reach the next county and a sky like a giant blue dome that is pinned to earth on far away corners, propped on distant forests or skating along the outermost sighting of ocean, sometimes juggled by twenty-foot swells so that the line is not curved or straight but

corrugated and living. The world must be full of such places
and yet, even I was to become a city-dweller. There was no
reason that I couldn't go home.

So the military didn't want me, a surrogate father saying, go
live, forget war. How many had the doctor been willing to save
through kindness, fatherly generosity, compassion? But then,
what must it have felt like to send boys off to the mud and
blood of Europe? It could have been duty or it could have
been something else. And for him to save me from an apocalypse I knew almost nothing about, he no doubt had to select
someone from that straggled line on Hollis Street to go off to
the training camps to learn about guns and the hardware of
killing and the designs inside men's minds that allowed for
mass murders of strangers.

But I was here in Halifax, returning a native son, blasted free
in one war, drawn back by another. I knew where our old
house had been and walked there almost with my eyes closed,
up George Street away from the harbour. Advertisements were
painted artlessly on the side of dirty brick buildings. Tobacco,
savings bonds, automobiles. The word *Chevrolet* stuck like a
jack-knife in my mind, conjuring up a world of affluence,
motion, fluid excitement and the joys of all things urban and
civilized. When I reached the corner where our house had
been, I found only rubble, not from the blast, of course, but
from men still at work tearing down the old city, hauling away
the stuff that was once my home. One machine was pushing
the foundation into the basement, another filling a truck that
was dumping the stuff across the street in a hole that probably
too was once a basement. I recreated the phantom of what my
house must have looked like and stared for a long while at
empty air, envisioning bedrooms and kitchen and exactly
what the floorboards must have felt like to my knees, and my
father in and out at odd hours to work at the docks, my mother
up at the crack of grey to begin a day, to keep me alive, to go
off teaching in that nearby school where she had been unlucky
enough to have stood in front of a window at the exact

devil allusion

moment a giant hand had reached up from the depths of the harbour and drawn those two ships together to crash and set off the explosion.

Halifax, a garrison town from the start and to the last, found old men grabbing ancient rifles after the disaster and walking down Quinpool toward the harbour ready to meet the Hun, ready to retake the Citadel if necessary. Families huddled on a frozen Commons in snow, and freezing rain waiting for the second attack, North America under siege at last. Some great betrayal had let the Germans into the mined harbour and here they were. No accident. People dying of pneumonia rather than staying inside a woodframe house about to be shredded from unseen enemies. So many died needlessly rather than getting back inside to restoke dying fires and resettle a shattered life.

Great clouds of birds had flown off in all directions, some having started even before morning, before the blast, forever marking in their collective memory the year and day of 1917, some flying to fields in Enfield, others east to the Shore, some to the South Shore and yet others flew straight to sea. The gulls survived, the migrants found their way back and others flew until they fell dead. At sea, a devoted watchman of the navy looked back toward his homeland and saw a black cloud of birds relentless on its run. At first, it hinted some strange advance of enemies from his own land; then he saw them to be birds, common starlings and sparrows and mourning doves and, before he could signal his captain to inform him of the strange phenomenon, they fell all at once into the sea almost at the bow of the ship. They floated, helpless, with wings outstretched and then sank like rocks, their collective strength gone, energy dissipated and purpose confused. Their counterparts who had stayed inland or gone down the coast survived.

Margaret, who had picked up being my mother as if it was the most natural thing to do, had said to me, "Dead by accident, dead by will, it amounts to the same. Best to keep out of harm's way." The trick was learning how.

If this was a new Halifax, a rebuilt city, it was a confused,
chaotic replica, all motion and activity, people snapping heels
up and down the hill, restless feet and minds that must have
had compass-like needles directing them to one place and
then another through some urban magnetism that kept everything moving rapidly. Watching them, I was overtaken by the
desire to be able to move like that. To have some place to go
. . . a job, a woman, a room to call my own, a movie maybe, or
a restaurant. To be one of them ricocheting around this
blackened noisy city, so self-important with its harbour full of
waiting ships wanting supplies, and men for the war, and
money changing hands all over town, people giving orders
and taking them, making do and making ends meet. The
confusion was so bright in my mind that I couldn't give it up.
The Shore seemed a million miles away and in a different
country. I had found my war and the battle was simply to
overcome what was me and become one of them. So I walked
up and down the hill dozens of times, cross-circuiting the city
from Water Street up to the Citadel then back to the wharves,
then the length of Gottingen, then down side streets where
kids sailed little boats of wood chips down a thawing gutter
and everywhere I went, I smelled things new. Somewhere in
town a chocolate factory perfumed the air and it was sicken-
ingly sweet but captivating. The essence came and went with
a shifting breeze and I tracked it down to a building where a
whistle blew and a door opened and a hundred women
dressed in heavy overcoats poured out a door and divided, like
a small militia headed off in two directions for attack. And
there were also smells of coal and oil, like grease in the air,
clinging to my nostrils, the fume of endless faces inhaling
cigarettes, puffing madly and with conviction, then electric
odours from overhead wires frying the very air as a streetcar
passed by, trucks puffing black clouds at us all as we walked
on and on, no one seeming to mind, some seeming to suck it
into their lungs with gusto as if this was what city living was all
about and exhaust was the very essence of existence. The smell
of foods cooking and cooked sometimes found their way to
me, all unfamiliar except for a zephyr of coffee that blew out

of some cafeteria window looking for me, reminding me of my own presence here at the centre of the crazy fury of living. I was almost happy.

My feet took me back down to the harbour where everything seemed even more fantastically frenetic and confusing. But it was here that I was most at home with the smell of rotting wharf wood and stale fish odours and the insistence of the wind off the sea, breathing up the harbour, blowing salt-clean air into the Narrows and making me feel light and dizzy and safe. Tugs were pushing and pulling warships around and the ferries continued to snake back and forth through the busy harbour traffic. I kept walking south down Water Street, where traffic seemed to crawl around in any direction, cars weaving in and out, trucks backing up three and four blocks at a time, other trucks unloading, cocked perpendicular to the traffic so that cars had to flow around and almost into each other. When I came to the place where the smells were most over-whelming, the stench of spoiled rotting fish and the avarice of coal smoke, I found an ugly blackstained brick wall with a notice. **Help Wanted/O'Leary's Fish**, a corroded metal sign said, the harbour having had at it through many storms.

Inside, a man thin as a pencil and to my mind almost faceless behind metal-rimmed glasses asked me if I could gut and fillet, only he said fill-eh, like in Chevrolet, so I knew him for a Yank and it was clear that he and I had not grown up within a light year of each other.

But I said, sure, when do I start?

Tomorrow. Already he was back studying a bunch of num-bers on a piece of paper, picking up a phone and mumbling something to someone on the other end. His office was a tiny cubicle with walls only halfway up to the ceiling and the whole place smelled of the deadest of dead fish ever extracted from the sea. Dead fish inside is never like dead fish outside where the sun and wind turn it into a queer sort of perfume. Here it smelled like John Kincaid's kitchen where his mother had cooked his old man's mackerel for three decades until it had varnished the ceiling, the walls and the windows in a green veneer that defied description. That kitchen had always smelled like the very breath of the dead to me. John had claimed he could never smell a thing and maybe he couldn't but I had still held onto the nerve endings in my nose and here I was in this immense gutting shed fifty times the size of Kincaid's kitchen and the smell of something that dead, that rotten, and the thought of an actual job with real money made my head swim. So my future was confirmed.

The rooming house was on Hollis, not far from where I had started out the tour. The room seemed cheap enough, everything in the place was cheap. It looked out over the brewery which seemed like the most unlikely building I had ever seen on earth. The whole neighbourhood had its own bouquet of melting cheese and burning ties that remained unexplained but unquestioned. I had a room with a cracked mirror and a window that somebody had thrown a rock through. The rock was still on the woven rag rug when I was introduced to my new home. Three walls had plaster, one didn't.

"You can have it if you wants," the landlady said. She treated me like I was invisible but I could see that was her way to treat people and underneath it I sensed something human, something maybe even warm for such a hulk as her. When she spoke, she always said, "If you wants to, it's up to you," after anything she said. I asked her what her name was. She just said, "You can call me Mrs. Whynacht, if you wants, it's up to you."

"Thank you, Mrs. Whynacht," I said. There was this great shyness about her and somehow those pounds of useless flesh she carried around like empty suitcases didn't suit her, made her eyes sit too far back inside the folds, made her mouth seem small and insignificant. I had this image of some slender, ambitious woman inside all that baggage, wanting to get out, someone with conviction and energy, but instead she was bound up inside an unwieldy body showing penny poor strangers empty rooms.

"You must be from here in Halifax, then?" I asked her as she was about to leave.

"I come from Lunenburg," she said, suddenly angry at my insult. "My husband's on one of the ships out of here. Better to be near him, when he's in, don't you think?" She had stepped out of herself, had become different, human, indignant.

"That's very wise of you."

"You ain't from the Sou' Shore yourself?"

"Eastern Shore."

"Oh." She was shutting down the conversation, folding herself back into the wrapping flesh, losing interest already. "Ya can stay as long as ya pay. One day, one mont' . . . if ya want. It's up to you."

"Thank you, Mrs. Whynacht."

At least I could watch the harbour from my room. A south swell was pumping wind chop up toward Bedford Basin and the tugs were spitting spray. The wall and window had so many air leaks that I could almost feel the spray on my face, feel the driving winds welcoming me to Halifax, to my room.

Mrs. Whynacht had not told me that I was living among entrepreneurs. The plasterless wall adjoined a room where commerce was in progress and it was like someone had a radio on in my room. I could hear the bargaining, the settlement of price, the business at hand and the settlement of accounts receivable. I was lying on my ratty horsehair stuffed bed, plotting exactly how much money I would be making from shredding fish guts over the next few months when the occupation of my neighbour sank in. My first reaction was to laugh out loud, soon after the first customer had abandoned the room.

" . . . the hell are you laughing at?" I heard a raspy voice curse at me through the wall. I half-expected her to bust through and clobber me with something. And I wondered what she must look like.

I said nothing at all but lay silent, afraid maybe that Mrs. Whynacht would receive a complaint that the new tenant was a snob, a man who insults women of trade. I just shut up.

I had been a hundred-percent right about the frantic pace of living in Halifax. Next door, things happened at a rapid clip. I was baffled that nothing seemed to take more than a few minutes. Doors opening and closing. Price quotes. Negotiations. Sometimes the negotiations took longer than the business.

Pretty soon a storm of ice pellets rattled machine gun chatter against my frail window and helped to subdue the noises next door. When it was over, I went out for a meal at a tiny shabby restaurant where a Portuguese woman wiped every knife, fork and spoon before she set them at my place. She couldn't speak English and indicated to me to just point to the number on the menu for whatever I wanted. I drank four cups of coffee and overstayed my welcome but left a big tip, the first time I had ever left a tip for anything in my life. When I returned to my room, it was cold and damp. A single twenty-watt bulb gave the place a sickly yellow pallor that made me feel like I was about to go to sleep in a glue bottle. Next door it was all quiet except for the sound of the woman snoring.

Doors flapped open like shotgun blasts all through the night and I could not adjust to the noise of toilets flushing. It confounded me that civilization with all of its conveniences could be so annoying, that people willed themselves to a life of rude awakenings, of machines roaring down streets at night, of pipes drumming in the dawn. Someone in this house must have had heat; a radiator beneath my window intimated a comforting purpose, but each time I tested its ambition it was stone cold.

In the morning there was no sign at all of the tenant next to my door. Aside from the snoring, I had not heard a stirring from that direction all night, although I confess I had lain there in my own bed waiting to hear someone move in their sleep, someone speak a shred of a dream; I had been anxious to see the face of someone who had such a profession, not out of moral rectitude but simply out of an eager curiosity. The door was slightly ajar, so I peeked in.

Nothing. It was like a crypt in there. A cracked window shade pulled three-quarters down, a bare bed frame, not even a mattress, just a coarse blanket on rusted springs and one cardboard closet tilting from a corner. But the heat was on. I went in, sat down on the springs and held my hands to the warmth of the baroque heater.

* * *

I thought the first hour on the job would kill me. The cold, the smell, the same dead questioning eyes of fish after fish under such alien ambiguous lights. Outside the sun was bold and clean, but in there it had been shut out by metal and boards, almost as if to remind us that we were set apart from the living, that we were part of this prison world. Our time was not our own until noon break and even then we had only twenty minutes, not a full half-hour. Aside from a couple of boys, I was the only male on the cutting floor. My knife was dull, and it took me ten questions before somebody took me to a stone for sharpening. Even then, the skeleton who had hired me came trailing in to say my work was what counted, not the gleam of my blade. I tried to explain the relationship of the two but all he said was, "Suit yourself. But it'll cost you."

The women were all heavy and wrapped in ragged clothes like Russian peasants. "Don't you pay him no mind," one said, meaning MacIver, the manager. "His wife won't sleep wid him. That's his problem." She had to keep reminding me that I was being too careful, that the trick was to speed things up, that it was piecework after all and a lot of this stuff was going off to Europe anyway. "People dere are probably starving to deat' anyways. Dey won't mind if you leaves a few bones for da cat." She reminded me some of Margaret but the big difference was that she was a city woman. She understood the way things were done here and she had a matter-of-fact air about her. The other "girls" called her Queenie and she did seem to have an air of leadership. I soon learned that her advice was worth listening to.

"You must have your own agonies, I s'pose, if dey turned you away," she said after a spell of quiet. She looped her knife inside the fish and slipped it up in one swift move, cutting and removing the guts in the blink of an eye.

"You mean the army? Just call it bad luck."

"Just the same, don't go lettin' dem over dere go suggesting a walk behind the ice shed." She swung her knife up over my head, dripping blood on my face, pointing to "dem over dere," younger women with hair tied up on top of their heads and wearing overcoats. They were packing cod into boxes that were then rolled down a line to the freezer. "You think you're bad off now; wait'll dey give you a little sumptin' to take along home wid you like a souvenir."

"Thanks for the advice," I told her, slowing down a bit too much, getting behind in my own work.

MacIver had come up from behind suggesting that maybe I should be told about the quota system. I didn't know what he meant but he walked on, went to talk to the girls stuffing boxes of cod, said something that made them laugh.

"Look at dat," said Queenie. "See what I mean. The man's scarcely human." She heaved about twenty "dressed" fish over into my pile to make my work look up to the women's standards. I thanked her and cut on, finding I wanted to sharpen my knife almost every twentieth fish as I would have back on the dock but I could see that it wasn't the way here. You cut with your arm, not your wrist. Queenie had forearms like iron and hands like the old fishermen from back home—leathery and white, callused almost wherever there was skin. For a while the stench of the place had gone away; I had been diverted by the bizarre sights of such a purgatory and the stench didn't catch up with me again until nearly noon. Somebody had opened a door. Clean air mixed with the dead and I wanted to throw up, but I kept it down. When I went out to the harbour at break, however, the nausea came back and I had to let go, puking all over the bulkhead with half the harbour-men there to watch. The gulls swooped down quick to clean up the mess, and I gave them as well the small lunch I had packed for their prompt janitorial services. When I went back in, I saw that most of the women had stayed right with their tables. The only ones missing were the boxing girls and the boys who had been working the machines.

Later, I overstayed my welcome at the sink in the bathroom back at the rooming house. Trying to wash off the day's work was clearly an impossible task. One of the tenants from downstairs was at the door banging and cursing to get in.

On my way back to my cave, I saw that someone was in the room next door. The battered door was half-open and I could hear the soft hum of a woman's voice, a sad Gaelic lilt, something so familiar but not to be placed, just beyond the threshold of identification. Dripping water and soap, still holding my hands up in the air as if I had just performed surgery, I tapped on the door.

A young woman appeared and stood, looking baffled, her soft warm face open and questioning. What did I want?

"I just wanted to say hello. We're neighbours." As I said the word, I felt absurd. At home, neighbours meant you lived within a day's walk or that your pastures met somewhere back in a foggy thicket far off from your home, or that your uncle's son had married someone else's niece.

"It's a pleasure." She held out her hand. I had never seen a woman do this before.

Not knowing exactly what to do, I kissed it. She pulled back, laughing. "Oh, I see. A gentleman. A gentleman who smells of the perfume of the sea."

"I'm sorry. I thought . . . " But I didn't know what I thought. Instead, I retreated to my own room. "It's nice to meet you," I said. My face was starting to glow red.

Lying on my rack in my cold room, I puzzled over her. Clearly she could not be the same one who had howled at me through the wall. But I could rest assured, Queenie had told me, that any lady I met in the house where I was staying was sure to be of the same stock. Queenie had thought I'd be better to spend as much time away from there as I could. She invited me to a Temperance meeting for that evening.

"Bloody Jesus," she told me, "the next thing you know, dey'll be wanting to let women into the Halifax taverns to drink along with the men. Not over my dead body!"

But I didn't go along to scoff with the other teetotalers at the ruin of alcohol. I lay stone-stiff and silent on my bed, fearing that I would hear what I expected from next door. My understanding of the world had been so schematic, so skeletal that I felt numb in my stupidity. Loneliness compounded confusion, and finally in a cold sweat, like a sleepwalker, I got up, put my clothes on and walked next door, paused, then knocked.

In a minute, I heard feet shuffling on the floor, then a lamp was lit. When the door opened, the first thing I noticed was the light of an oil lamp, not the caustic metal light of electric bulbs. The young woman was standing at the door in a long flannel nightdress, a soft warm glow creating a halo in the frizzing ends of her hair.

"I guess your business must not be so good tonight. I wondered how much it would be to stay the night with you." I saw myself saying the words as if I was watching some ghost figurine of me from the hallway ceiling, as if I was operating the mouth muscles like the strings of a puppet.

Her sleepy, warm expression knotted into a frown and before I said more, the door slammed hard in my face, harder on my hand that had been braced on the door frame. I didn't scream. Neither did she. I pulled my hand free and went back to my room nursing two injured fingers through a long, black cold night. Later that night I heard the sound of fire engines for the first time in my existence. A church had burned down somewhere in the North End while a late winter storm howled down, driving snow horizontal along Hollis Street, piling up on windows and sticking until there was nothing to see but the insistent white angry blindness of winter.

* * *

May 7, 1945. It could have been that the fingers were broken but, if so, I deserved it. A lousy night's sleep I had, sinking deeper into unresolvable loneliness. Having met Eleanor for just one brief moment, I was hopelessly attracted to her. Her very presence beyond the ravaged wall made my own life seem dismal and pointless. I had not really meant what I said to her, but it was an attempt to be a man of the world; someone who could speak in urban Halifax ways. But I had assumed the unassumable and blundered like a fool. Eleanor was not the same as the former tenant and I had missed the obvious. Even if she had been less of a lady and more of what I had expected, I would have felt the same. I'm no moralist when it comes to love.

An empty room, a cold night for May, the North still hunkering down and spilling cold arrogance around the knees of the city. The world was changing that night, and I hadn't been paying attention to anything outside the private arctic of my room, the throbbing of my fingers and the eulogy in my ears. In the morning, I left before it was light, walked around the desolate streets and rambled around the damp wharves where the old men still prepared to head out past the harbour mouth for a day's catch. Like other days, there were no young men, except those in uniform who dangled cigarettes from their lips and looked cocky, self-important and rigid.

At work, Queenie was trying to tell me something. She was worked up and flustered, going on about the war. According to her it was about to end, at least in Europe. "Good God, look out for your loved ones then," she said. "The boys'll be tearing the city apart brick by brick and none of the women will be safe." Then she sneered over toward her adversaries, the boxing girls, and added "'ceptin' them." The girls saw she was talking to me about them and waved. I didn't smile or wave, just kept on trying to manage my cutting knife, dull and uncooperative. And now my numb fingers had a hard time sliding it through the cod's guts. With a mind of its own, it struck out for human blood, finding the palm of my good hand and gouging across it, suddenly sharp and new like the devil had taken the wield of it. I gushed blood and Queenie let out a yell. She wrapped her scarf around it and told me to press in hard. "Now look. You get out of here right quick

before himself sees you with the damage. He likes to fire
people for clumsiness but if he don't see it, I'll tell him it was
sompthin' else. You run along. Find a hospital or a doctor and
let 'em clean out the fish scales."

I took her advice and made an exodus. The saltwater and
fish slime felt hot and savage on my new wound as I made my
way back to the boarding house. The city had changed radi-
cally since morning. Everything was in motion. Everyone was
talking. Some shopkeepers were already closing up for the
day, a few were nailing boards over doors. I was very curious
and suddenly it struck me that my own sense of the war coming
to an end was all wrong, that perhaps the Allies had suddenly
lost ground and Halifax was about to be invaded. The fear had
always been with this garrison city.

I hurried on, ran into my building, up the creaking flight of
stairs and into the bathroom where I ran icy water over my
hand. The blood was still coming and as I looked out in the
hallway, I could see that the soaked scarf had dripped a trail,
probably across the city as I had made my way. A door opened
and Eleanor saw me standing there, pale and bleeding. She
walked back into her room and came out with a pillowcase.
Without speaking, she took my hand and examined the cut. I
could see now that it was a long slice and not extremely deep
but it bled well, as if it wanted all the blood out of me as soon
as it was able. She dried it as best she could, wrapped the
pillowcase and then pressed down hard with her own small
delicate hands. "You better lie down in your room, so you
don't pass out. You've probably lost a lot of blood." Her voice
was totally foreign to me—mannered, educated and above all,
gentle. She led me back to my room and closed the door
behind her.

"And I suppose you'd like to freeze to death as well," she
chastised. She went over to the cold radiator and turned a
knob near the floor. I could hear hot water dancing up the
pipes into the near-frozen contraption. It was a wonder I had
survived my few days in the city.

"A man likes to fight, I guess." She motioned to my hand.

"Oh, no. Nothing like that. My fingers didn't work so good and I slipped with a knife. At work. At the fishplant." She was standing over me as I lay down. The softness in her had been held back by something, her mistrust of me, her distaste for what she thought violence. Then it pushed back through the mask of propriety she had been holding up.

"I'm sorry. You had frightened me."

"I deserved it."

The room had filled with something. She had changed the place. It took on an aura of something almost spiritual. I might have been light-headed from the loss of blood, but it was more than that. Everything I lay my eyes upon glowed with a new inner life beyond anything I had ever known. I thought of every poet I had ever read and words came back. Things I once thought to be maudlin and sentimental now seemed vital and important.

People were yelling in the streets. Car horns were blowing. Somebody raced by in a horse-drawn carriage, the sound of the hooves like hard, frozen rain falling on a metal roof. Downstairs, men were pounding on the door, then I heard footsteps running up the stairs, knocking on doors. They knocked on Eleanor's and she got up to go see who it was, but I pulled her back and she looked puzzled. They knocked again, then simply went in, circled the small room, two, maybe three men, sounding like someone had led a bull into the place.

"Wouldn't you know it. The bloody bitch ain't here." They knocked something over then left, pushing at each other, laughing, grumbling, spitting on the floor and heaving an empty bottle in the bathroom. Eleanor looked frightened now. Down on Hollis Street, the first window broke and somewhere toward Province House a woman screamed. Others were cheering. Two cars collided and a few more windows were being smashed. The war in Europe was over. The war had once again come home to Halifax for a day.

"Don't worry. They weren't looking for you. The girl who had the room before you. I think they were looking for her."

I preferred not to say anything else. She seemed to understand. Bridges were being built between us. I was afraid to say too much for fear I would destroy the construction at hand.

"Stay put. I'll be right back." She went into her room and came back with a square cardboard box with holes punched in it. Inside was an injured sparrow she had found the day before when it had tried to smash itself to death on a window of one of the bank buildings. "I think he's getting better," she said, placing it near the now-warm radiator. Then she returned to her room again and came back with a tiny stove that used canned fuel. She lit a match and set a pot of water on to boil, all in the centre of the dirty hardwood floor. When the water had boiled, she poured us each a cup of tea into two china cups. The tea was hot and bitter and tasted like the most precious fluid that had ever touched my lips. Without speaking she closed the lid on the can of fuel, and simply sat there on the bare floor in a dress more suited to summer than a damp cold day in May. I wanted to say so much but had the good sense to keep my mouth shut and fall asleep. Later she said that me falling asleep was one of the most satisfying things she had ever seen. And I never truly knew what she meant by it. When I woke up it was late afternoon. The room was warm for the first time and the sun had bullied its way through the cloudy smudged glass in the panes in the window.

"I think he's ready for a test flight," Eleanor said, more to the bird than to me.

I sat up, and let the dizziness clear, then went over and pushed up the window. Eleanor set the bird gently on the ledge and we moved back, not wanting to hurry it. He looked around, confused between inside and outside, having known only the outer face of buildings before. Then, as if someone had thrown a switch, he was off, out and up, flying above the smoke-stained buildings and remembering what an open sky did to pump life through wings and make a man-made world shrink back to its proper place.

As Eleanor and I looked out the window, leaning on our elbows, we saw the city being torn apart. Navy men, men in other uniforms were thrashing about, fighting each other, knocking over trash cans, trying to roll over a police car. Smashing glass provided a background for gunshots and screaming. Halifax was being ransacked in celebration. With no further conquests, the domestic military force had turned back on its own city and was tearing the place apart. It was the happiest day of my life.

✓ stupid

The Fields of Heaven

A whale beached at the foot of the hill today. It was alive, suffering—stupefied by the machinations of the world like all of us. The sun was bright and my pigeons were tripping out the windows from the rusting automobiles where they live. All those cars are like the itinerary of a life, the remains of boyhood/manhood dreams, empty hulks, happily rusting away under a savage sun while birds nest inside them on eggs, hatching hungry mouths that want life, want the cycle. But always there would be hungry hawks and inland eagles waiting to carve their own lives from the blood of the living.

Below me at the edge of a calm, retreating sea, the whale was sprawled like a great blue-grey boulder, a living rock among dead stones, one unblinking eye locked onto the empty sky, not the eye of the dead, but the sceptic's eye of a creature lured from the safety of the deep with the promise of something better, only to find itself dashed and foundering, and now fearing the worst: a dry death.

I ran shoeless to the precipice then down the path that was no path, for the hill is constantly changing, patches of weed, tufts of grass sliding a slow descent to the bottom on the exposed hillside. The hill had conspired sharp igneous knives to come to the surface, the rain having pulled back the mulch and left brittle edges waiting to bloody frail feet. The pain was something I could understand. I had never truly seen a beached whale but had heard the stories. Always, they said, the whale would return if hauled loose, to flap again on the shore and inflict his rotting carcass on the people on land. As I descended, I locked onto the eye; it blinked. Life, purpose, reason to push dying mammals back into safety.

The eye meant life. Without it, I saw nothing but a blob of creature flesh, cold, inanimate, but the eye held in the sky, took in the approach of a two-legged creature with shortening breath and cursing steps down a gravelly hill toward it. The whale saw an impossibly thin, almost reptilian pale-fleshed animal with white hair nearly down to its shoulders, with a coarse stubbled chin like something chiselled from rock. He saw the man stumble, curse again, use hands like feet to flap through air and then it was there, standing over him, filling up the sky, demanding attention, wanting something, talking a noise unsuccessful in an ocean of air. Part of it reached out and touched him on the surface, the hand like a burning sun, scorching in its own heat. Then it cupped water from a pool and danced moisture on his head.

I kept hauling and splashing. The eye blinked more. The body heaved in a slow pulse. A light breeze was coming up off the land, warm and salt-free. That was the worst that could happen. Dry, inland wind. That and a retreating tide. Hands were not buckets and whale mountains were not to be moved. More would have to be done. Contact first. The whale must understand. Understand what? I wasn't sure, simply that I wouldn't give up. I would give it my best try. Up above, my birds circled, insisting on the absolute of living, of the restlessness of living things, the need to move, to make avenues through air, through water, to pump blood and life every minute. I unbuttoned my shirt and put my chest up against the whale. My heart was racing from the downhill scree jump and I was sure the whale would understand. The pumping of a heart, the rhythm of a beating muscle pushing blood around inside an old man. I remained like that for five minutes, then went to the tidal pool closest and splashed water on the burning beast like a reckless, ancient fireman. I kept at it until I knew the sun and wind were getting ahead of me. Then I scrambled up the hill and ran the quarter-mile to Kenzie's house.

I barged in, found him recovering from a drunk and bashed him around a bit, told him to get up, I wanted his help, I needed his dory. Kenzie didn't like the rude deportation from whatever world he had been in, but he knew it was me and that I wouldn't be there without good reason. I told him to come around the point in his dory, bring blankets, buckets. He understood and I knew he would do it. Right after he puked his guts out in the sink. But he would be there as quick as any man. Kenzie loved things living, loved life so bad he pushed death away every morning with two hands, swallowed life in great gulps and paid his daily price for living. And I trusted him more than any other man still living within reach. Others, the new fishers, with bigger boats and engines and sonar that peeped into the bedrooms of the deep, were men of money who had killed whales and seals before for an extra pocketful. The government paid them still to kill grey seals. The government would say it protected the whales, but not well enough. I couldn't trust helicopters with grappling hooks to try to tow the creature free. And somewhere in the Halifax paper, I had seen a picture of a bulldozer on a beach near Parrsboro trying to bury a beached whale just to cover up the stench. Better to let two men and a beast go at it alone, poker face against death, ignorant of what a body can do and what it can't do.

Half-running, half-walking back to the old cart track, scalloped by car wheels into two deep ruts and painted green just recently by the late but confirmed arrival of summer, I wanted Eleanor here to share the salvation of the whale with me. I wanted it so bad, it came up from behind like a mugger with a heavy rock and it brought me down to my knees, pushing itself green and living into my chest while my head reeled and I sucked in a sob. She had been forgotten for a full hour. I had been a person alone with a crisis. And then she was back, with me, present again by her terrifying absence. This time when the tears came, it hurt. I hadn't let them loose for days and when they broke my mental lock on their glands, there were sharp spasms of pain in both eyes and I feared that it wouldn't stop. But I pushed one hand down into the soggy rut and another and then my knees wanted up. I stumbled on. What I felt toward saving the whale now was something new, something that was so much less of me and more of Eleanor I realized that she had left me this gift, locked inside and waiting to come out at this minute. What I felt for saving the whale was the stuff that Eleanor had been made of, a wife whose compassion for the hurt, the maimed, the destitute had been so strong that I had sometimes thought it would have torn our marriage apart. Her need to comfort had been indomitable and whatever had needed saving she had always saved. Now, she had given me her power to heal.

I scrambled down the cliff, this time with shoes, with blankets, with an old canvas bag that carried heavy rope, and an old hydraulic car jack. I heaved two galvanized buckets down ahead of me, then startled by the racket they made bashing themselves on the rocks, I looked down to see that I was not alone. A young woman had appeared. I had met her once before when she had shown up earlier this year. Maybe twenty years old. All softness and smiles, then.

The greedy sea that had taken so much from all of us these years had gone crazy now with presenting things to me. What was left of Kincaid, then the whale, now the girl again. Retribution. Apology. But always in confused forms, things half-dead, half-living, things starved and stranded between two worlds like I was myself. But this was different. Here she was, more alive than anything I had ever seen, a soother of stranded creatures herself. The girl saw my equipment and smiled.

"I think this one's only a baby. How long has he been out there?"

"I don't know. He wasn't here this morning."

"I don't think they can last more than a few hours."

"Damn."

She frowned at my word. Tide would be on its way in in two hours, not high again until six hours after that. Even then I wasn't sure the tide would come up high enough to loosen the massive weight from the rocks.

"We gotta save him," she insisted. I knew she was right but wondered what she would think if we actually succeeded, only to find him turn and ram for the rocks again as they were wont to do. Pessimism was for old men. I said nothing about it. As she looked at me for some sort of answer, I filled up from the inside with something warm, said simply, "We'll do it." There was no choice.

*   *   *

We soaked the blankets in the sea and tossed them over the creature and he moved—his whole frame heaved. How could he know for sure whether we were there to save or to kill? The girl said nothing to me but picked up my bucket and began splashing sea water on the blankets while I sat down by the eye, wanting it to know what I knew. I had seen so many things die in sixty-nine years. A mother, a father, a way of life and the dreams that went with it. I had been so sure some things could not change, that the city would have stayed where it was rather than crawling like a living thing itself north and east to chew up farms and wreck simple lives.

Dead moles in a garden at sunup, dead sparrows on the grill of an old Ford, a frozen cat in a storm drain in Halifax, the sight of a fireman hauling the charred remains of John Kincaid out of the bitch's house on a cold clear night when the stars pulled down close to plant cold kisses on your cheeks. Then Eleanor, asleep one minute, quiet with warm love in an old man's arms, and then suddenly she's gone, slipped off to nowhere or somewhere leaving a great hollow core in the world. A simple thing, a common thing for a man to lose a wife, nothing certainly for the world to take notice of, but a tragedy much greater than all the world wars. I would have traded the very durability of the planet for another hour to have held her just like that, for her body to stay warm, for her breathing to sing its harmony close in my ears and keep me clear of the barbed nightmares to come.

A hand was touching me. The girl. She saw the tears tracking down my cheeks. *God. An old fogey, senile, worthless, wallowing in God knows what sort of reverie.* I was pretty pathetic. Thinking maybe it was time to get me out of the way, let the living get on with the living. Call up the Coast Guard, call in the helicopters, the tugs. Or get it over with quick; go bring in men with chain saws and flailing tools, carve away. Save the oil, throw away the meat, find the heart and drive a harpoon through it. Do something practical, make the suffering short; that's the modern way. No time to wait for tides, for the slow ambitions of a planet whose seas are ruled by a moon hung far out there in space. Get on with it. Clean it up. You don't want to have to smell the rot. Then gather up the bones and ship them back to Queen Victoria. Whalebones for great domed dresses, whalebones conspiring with textiles to cover up the flesh, to civilize, to build up difficult walls against passions and lust. Go on, kill him now, quick, before she finds out that he'll want death again as soon as he's free. A defect of evolution; he's no different than us. You heard the news. Syria, Lebanon, MX, Cruise, megatons for the good, for the common good. Even an old man has ears for bad news pumped at him around the clock. A lot of tax money goes into the CBC to be sure that we hear all the bad news. Death is so important, so much fun, so relevant.

The eye stares up at an empty blue sky, the eye of God (a poet would have said) looking back in a vacant stare. The eye sees but it's independent now from the mind. The God who created this world, challenged His intellect for variety, for potential, then gave up and left the flaws, watched and watched, grew tired of it like a soap opera that overstays its network welcome. Then the viewer simply moved on to something else. He sees but he lingers not. The sky is hollow and blue and empty like the fields of heaven. His radiance still pours down from above on a day like this but without reason. The planet has shaped itself into consciousness and performs cruel tricks like this disposal of the whale; it pushes season after season and rides winds around the knees of civilization and will grow ice teeth back when it gets ready, great frozen molars that will chew cities back to rubble if men don't create their own collective suicide first. But I would trust the cruel compassion of nature over that of my own species, any day. She has been slow to perfect her weapons since God has abandoned her like an unwanted mistress. We have been quick and to the point. And now, we hold back, only for fear that the fun will be over too soon.

My eyes are open but blind as I feel her come near me, bend down on her knees and kiss me on the lips. When I can see, the sky is not empty but filled up with her soft young face, her hands cupping mine and her hair a golden brown fan caught on my coarse, wool shirt, a delicate curtain in a gentle breeze. She tells me that her name is Kelly.

"Thank you."

"Come on. We have work to do." She was straight to the point. I accepted the pointlessness of the big picture one more time and became optimistic at smaller, more important tasks at hand. I hauled and poured as if I wanted to drain the sea dry. Toward the hard edge of the horizon, I could see the bigger boats stationary, probably hauling up lobster traps by the dozen. But around the point I could also see Kenzie on the flat sea pulling oars, looking like a water spider governed by surface tension and jerking legs, skating along the calm blue glass with hard pulls. I wanted to know so much about the young woman before even Kenzie arrived, why she was there, where she had come from, what she was doing with her life.

"Tell me everything," I said.

* * *

I helped Kenzie get the lines of the boat attached loosely around the whale by wading in and out through the mussel pools, up to my knees in rockweed and kelp. I would walk two feet, slip and fall, get up, slide again on the kelp, then move on. It was quite a dance. Kenzie stayed in the boat, fortified by a pint of lemon gin and keeping his heavy shirt on despite the fact that a land breeze had lifted the temperature beyond eighty-five degrees. The tide had started in ever so slowly, carelessly, the sea unconcerned as usual about the difference between life and death. There had been no storms and the moon was at the wrong phase; it wouldn't be a particularly high tide, but it would have to do.

Kelly was still hauling buckets of seawater from the pools and splashing the whale. Kenzie had brought us about twenty old tins of sardine and herring that he kept in a cupboard for half a century probably and we had tried to force-feed the beast to no avail, his taste being somewhat off for fish in mustard and oil. Around noon, a helicopter flew low, the Coast Guard on a leisurely mission down the shore. But he flew on without seeing us and it was just as well. My pigeons had been ascribing larger and larger circles overhead and when the chopper had pulled in low, they shot off toward the northeast, fearing the noise and the maniacal spinning blades.

Kelly, I had learned, was a student at the Art College in Halifax and was spending the summer camping in a tent. Alone. She was wandering (hiking she had said) the Eastern Shore and loving every minute of it. When I had met her before she was on her way toward Wine Harbour and now she was headed back but she was thinking about staying around here for a while. "It's not easy to give all this up for living in the city." Each time she looked at me, I dissolved before her. As we talked, she reinforced again for me the fact that I was not just an old man, I was still human, still intact mostly, on the outside. We both felt driven to do everything to save the whale; it didn't seem such an impossible task.

"You know what he might do even if we get him off the rocks and he's still alive?" I asked her, wanting to be sure she was aware of the worst.

"He'll try to swim back here and bash himself on the rocks again. They say it's something that goes wrong in the brain. Sometimes there's no way to stop them. It's not an error in judgement. It's a decision."

"How do you know that?"

"Books. I've read lots. Too many."

I had also read too many books, filled my head with explanations and reasons, buried myself in the fanciful minds of poets and philosophers. But I was never a reader of science.

"Then it's hopeless after all?" I asked. Suddenly it occurred to me that she was staging this whole rescue attempt to satisfy me. I was the naïve believer that we could save a creature bent on self-destruction. I was touched, then angered. She saw my expression change.

"Decisions can be reversed. We not only have to do the saving. We have to do the convincing."

The tide was finally up at least a foot over the crusty rocks and the seaweed began to gently pull itself backwards and forwards in the tiny waves. You would get maybe five days out of a summer like this: the sea was more Caribbean than North Atlantic, the way it looked at least, blue and clear and almost sexy in its tranquil vitality. Kenzie had grown tired of the wait in the hot sun and had fallen asleep at the oars. His dory slipped sideways up to the rocks and bumped there until I waded over to help him out, leading him to a soft sandy spot high above the tide's reach where he gratefully collapsed into a childlike sleep. It reminded me of putting my own son into his bed so many years before, the soft rhythmic sound of breathing on my shoulder and the expressionless, distant face of one oblivious to the battles of the waking world.

We didn't want to move the whale until the tide was at its peak for fear of tearing him apart on the barnacle rocks and at that we didn't want to move too slowly for fear the fickle tide would reverse itself as soon as it pleased and all hope would be lost. I hauled more rope so that a balanced network looped around the whale and he could not slip out until we wanted him to. When the time came. I was at the oarlocks and Kelly stationed by the whale, pushing as if her frail light frame could displace a ton of ocean mammal. Kenzie was not to be wakened. Maybe we should have sought more men, but I didn't know if fifty men would have done more good. It was like Kelly and I both wanted our innocence and optimism to prevail. We had seen the whale start to squirm as the waves washed around his mouth. He still had life, he still wanted the fullness of his own environment; he wanted to return to his world. There was no sign at all of another of his kind, a mother. He had perhaps been abandoned too young, this monster child, with a mother sending him to wash up on a mottled shore because she had sensed something wrong in him, some defect. He appeared to be alone but it didn't mean he couldn't live.

I pulled on the oars. The ropes drew tight like strings on a violin brought into perfect tune after years of disuse. I felt my own muscles tighten up as I heaved.

Even though I wasn't making headway, I knew the whale could feel the tug on it every time I cranked back hard on the oars. Kelly was almost up to her stomach in sea and I was half-fearful that she might get caught under the massive weight, so I shouted for her to swim out and join me. Maybe our friend would get the hint and want to join us too.

Kelly swam out through the setting sun, across the still, silent sea as I kept tension on the ropes. Her hair floated out in a wonderful trail behind her and she seemed so at home in the water that I couldn't help but think of mermaids I'd seen in books where drowned sailors sit on the floors of oceans and see fantastic feminine creatures swimming toward them for comfort. Once in the boat, we pulled together on the oars, me fearing for the longevity of the rusty oarlocks, but myself renewed in strength by the feeling of Kelly wet and warm beside me. Steadily we kept pulling on the oars until we had pulled the moon up out of the sea to shed cold silver light on us. As if on cue, the whale rolled free of the bottom and we were knocked out of our reverie, collapsing into each other like two spent lovers. The muscles in our arms were almost useless.

He rolled again and, as soon as we understood, we pulled hard once more in long, deep, smooth strokes, each of us holding both oars and rowing together.

Kelly changed suddenly. "Let's not give him a chance, dammit." She almost knocked me over as she began to drive the oars like someone possessed. I got the point. If we were to save him now, we had to row him hard toward the arcing moon, to the deepest water before he had a chance to get enough strength back to renegotiate his charter with death. Each of us on an oar now, we dragged hard to the dead weight; it was like trying to pull up the bottom of the sea to turn the world inside out. From the shore I heard Kenzie let out a hoot. "Thar she blows!" he screamed.

"This isn't exactly my idea of a Nantucket sleighride," Kelly said and I laughed.

"You *have* read a lot of books."

"*Moby Dick* was my least favourite."

The stern dug in deep like we were plowing a rut in the water. We made headway by inches as the whale squirmed in the ropes, with us or against us, there was no way of knowing. After maybe two more hours (it was hard to tell) we were clear of my headland. Ships could be seen miles off at sea, buoy markers to the right and left marking Rat Rock, Roaring Bull and Seething Scuttle. I had no idea of the source of my strength for I had been rowing for possibly five straight hours against the proclivities of gravity, inertia and stasis. The world wanted dead things to lie still. We would have none of it. Kelly stopped rowing suddenly and kissed me hard on the mouth, her own lips chapped and cracked, her breath salted and warm. She wanted to make sure I didn't give up. And I knew I wouldn't. We rowed until the sun was gone.

Finally we were at sea, far enough so that the shoreline looked to be a line of scattered carnival lights. I let go of the oars and slipped down into the boat ready to sleep or die or fade into oblivion. Kelly had stopped rowing but sat to watch the whale as it lay near the surface, not struggling, but flexing in its giant way and now, at last, blowing water out of the top. A good sign. I fell asleep then, waiting for nothing more.

When I woke up, I could barely move. My arms had been donated to the Salvation Army. The feeling was gone in them until I thrashed about and found the will to bring them back to life. Kelly was slumped over, still holding a single oar as the other dangled in the sea. She was crying and I knew at once the problem. We were drifting toward land, trailing after a sluggish but determined whale wanting back his beach.

I attacked the oars again with the vigour of the devil himself. We were not to be outdone. Kelly wrapped her arms around my back and together we pulled. At best we could create a stalemate. For a while we gave some ground, then shortly found it back as the whale, still exhausted, half-dead, faded in its own strength.

The new day grew hot and absolutely still and at something close to noon, the planet had stopped spinning. Everything had wound down. Kelly and I were both lying in the bottom of the dory once more, asleep, and the whale seemed to float, dead or alive, we couldn't tell.

We woke, our skin caked in salt, hot, cracked and burning from the sun, then looked up to see thin trailing wisps of clouds above us, dancing toward land. But when I sat upright, there was still no wind at all. We were being towed out to sea.

The whale stopped stone still when I dove down with a penknife to cut it free. He surfaced and I pulled myself up on him to get my lungs back. When it was all done, I swam around and looked straight in that giant eye and said something I can't remember now, something corny and stupid. And then he arced wide around the boat and moved off to the southeast and safety.

_____What Nora Thought She Saw

What Nora thought she saw was me with no clothes on in my kitchen, sitting bolt upright with my back flat against the snaky maple grain of a slatted wooden chair, me all skin and bone, pale as milk but for a sunburnt face and two arms red as lobster claws from two days at sea in a dory trying to haul some fool whale back to the deep. When I smiled at Nora, I thought my face would like to crack, splitting itself in half to let the other me out. I had white patches of dried sea salt corrugating along my forehead and drying up on my shoulders and I was feeling the way you should feel when you're dead tired but you're not gone because something has slapped new wind in your sails. Maybe you could last forever like that if you could just hold onto whatever insane thing had taken you over. I was in my own kitchen somewhere near noon without a stitch on me and some young woman from the Art College was attempting to reconstruct this ancient bag of bones on paper with a couple of old carpenter pencils and a charred piece of wood.

This is what Nora thought she saw and maybe she knew she was seeing it, but she was so used to seeing any number of strange things that were real or fanciful and this fit somewhere in between so she just accepted as she had learned to accept all things. Like Nora's cousin, Esther, would say about her: "What Nora thinks she sees and she actually sees are two different things, you better believe that."

And most people did. Except for Nora who believed everything she saw. And with good reason.

"Sit down, Nora, and pour some tea."

"You're looking good yourself," Nora told me as she followed the path worn into the floorboards, the soft valleyed highway going from door to woodstove to table. She had a habit of adding bits and pieces to what you said to her too, but she always did it in her head. It was like having an extra set of ears, she'd say. You hear the first part with the outside ears and then you'd hear the rest with the pair inside. When she had tried to look it up in an anatomy book she came across the term, *inner ear*, and she was convinced then and there that she knew what she was talking about. Most folks just didn't know how to use them. Same went for the eyes, Nora said.

Nora didn't say hello to Kelly, who had been trying to make herself invisible inside the drawing she was working on so intently and silently. Nora picked up on that right away and couldn't see Kelly there at all.

Just before Eleanor died, Nora had come over to tell us that she had been sitting around looking at a snow drift and saw Eleanor driving our old pink Nash Metropolitan through a brilliantly lit ice cave.

Eleanor sat at the wheel smiling while in front of the car was a magnificent snowplow truck sending out spumes of soft white billows. But it was definitely a tunnel where the walls were milk-white ice, translucent so that they seemed to be lit from within. Eleanor had the windshield wipers on to fend off the white spray from the snowplow and she had the radio on to a country and western station while beside her on the seat apparently were two large Canadian geese who didn't make a sound.

"I can remember that you didn't have no rust at all on the Nash," Nora had stated matter-of-factly, "and that Eleanor couldn't really see past the plow truck, but somewhere toward the end of the tunnel was the brightest, coldest light you ever wanted to see. But I lost the picture, see, and everything changed. I looked up at the sky above me and two geese were coming down out of the sky to land on the inlet. And I guess they didn't want to make some noise."

Eleanor and I had both laughed rather loudly. But not at Nora, at her story. Nora was one of us and had been for a long time, a lunatic and a visionary. One of the gentlest people I had known other than Eleanor.

Kelly was still invisible to Nora. I could see that she was finished with sketching me, so I proceeded to put my clothes back on. She had turned and was doing Nora now with the same intensity, her face focussing with such power as if to gather in every bit of light bounding off the old woman, collecting it and storing it in her drawing in some mysterious way. As I pulled up the suspenders, Nora tried to explain about the latest phase she was going through with her visions.

"I was in town the other day and here's this man carrying a stark naked woman over his shoulder, hauling her down Agricola Street. I tells my mother to look at that and she explains that it's just a mannequin he's carryin' and it don't mean nothin'. But then here you are today in your starkers and I'm wondering what it is they are trying to tell me. What, with all the nakedness cutting loose every which way I look."

It seems that Nora had been sitting down to a tin of herring in mustard oil the other Saturday and Jesus Christ had appeared to her in the altogether just to inform her that she was welcome back into the fold if she still cared. He had appeared just once before three years ago, fully clothed in a three-piece suit asking her politely to take up atheism if she didn't mind, things being a bit overly crowded in Christendom for the time being, and space being at a premium. Nora said she had complied, but now that He had come back in the form of a nudist, she was having other doubts of the faith.

"It don't seem to be quite right going through a nakedness phase like this at my age. The human body ain't got any mysteries to me any more since I gave up old John Kincaid."

Nora would have tried to marry John way back there before we all bumped twenty had it not been for the fact that he had acquired the habit of chewing tobacco as soon as he started doing so well with the cod. And it wasn't even really the tobacco that bothered her but the spitting. "I can't abide a man who spits," she said. It was one of the few judgements she ever made against anyone. "All that hawkin' and spackin' each way you turn your head. Just didn't think I could live with it. Even though there was John Kincaid, handsome like somebody had chipped him out of rock. I don't know. He might not have wanted me."

That was before the visions had started to come more regularly and before Kincaid had knotted himself up into his own private bowline. If Kincaid hadn't hated my guts, I might have done something about it—brought the two together. But in the end, Nora, in the full blossom of her bosomy youth, started to see ballet dances in the sunset and Kincaid went back to sea, to chew and spit and fish himself into oblivion.

It seemed crazy to watch the Shore filling up with so many single people, not marrying, but each one caught up in a private whirlpool of something or other. You'd think loneliness was out there huckstering door to door and making good commission as each one became a caricature of what he once was. But look at me. Who am I to talk now that I am sixty-nine with a dead wife? A neighbour comes by and finds me sitting naked in a hardwood chair while a college girl makes drawings. The world has been turned upside down and had its pockets emptied.

I can't say Nora was an unhappy person. She had dialogue on occasion with a handful of invisible cronies who she referred to as her guides. Once when I asked her what they looked like, she rooted around in a drawer and came up with a photograph of four actors and one actress who had appeared together in the Cecil B. DeMille film, *The Greatest*

Show on Earth. "Only they don't always look so grim," she said.
"One of 'em chews gum and the lady don't wear nearly as
much makeup. But that's them. Not one of 'em ever spit in
my presence."

When Nora had been six years old she had fallen down the
well at her home. It was a shallow well, only about eight feet
deep and, it being a dry summer, there wasn't more than a
couple of feet of water in it but Nora had hit her head on the
way down and blacked out. After several minutes had gone by,
her father, Edgar Dunphy, pulled her up feet first and she was
nearly blue. They thought they had lost her but she came back
to them and talked for three days without hardly ever shutting
up. After a while she quieted down and went back to school
telling everybody that she had died and come back, that her
time wasn't up on earth. Aside from that event where she had
received an introduction to her guides, things went fairly
normal until one day she was looking at the teacher, Miss
Eaton, and suddenly she saw nothing but a skeleton standing
at the blackboard hard at work on an addition problem. Nora
screamed and ran outside where she locked herself in the
outhouse until her guides showed up and talked her back to
being herself. Nora didn't tell anyone what she had seen until
Miss Eaton was sent off to Halifax with a tragic disease of the
bones. After that, Nora asked her guides to lighten up a bit,
that she didn't mind visions, but that she'd be damned if they
were all going to end up like this. Apparently the guides were
willing to undertake some degree of censorship in order to
keep Nora relatively sane for sixty-some years.

Nora was another one who had filed by on a regular basis to
sit in the kitchen and talk with Eleanor. Sometimes they'd sit
together on the back steps and watch the pigeons swirl around
up above. "We all should've had wings," Nora had reported
one day. "My guides pointed that out to me. It was only by
mistake that we were given fingers instead of feathers. Now it's
too late." She had seemed genuinely disappointed, sitting
there staring at her fingers that were long and delicate like
the tips of pigeon wings. Then following the birds with her

eyes out over the sea, she saw one of them arc wildly away from the flock and turn into a small dart-like airplane that vectored straight into the water. "Now you know, that ain't right, " she said.

Eleanor had called me over and we went out in the boat, the one I had made out of marine plywood according to the plans in a magazine. The water was so clear you could see the lobsters scrambling along the bottom and sure enough we came to the spot and there was something down there. You could see the shape of an old airplane and a propeller. The sea was quite shallow, maybe only twenty-five feet, but the colour of the machine was the colour of everything else on the bottom. The sea had tried to camouflage things. If it hadn't been for Nora I might've gone over that spot a thousand times and seen nothing but swaying rockweed, kelp and stones. Whatever happened there had happened a long time ago and was probably nobody's business. That's what I told them, but Eleanor would have none of it. She called up the Navy who sent out a helicopter that lowered some divers into the water.

That helicopter sat dead in the air like thunder with hummingbird wings, while men with masks and tanks rooted around. I had always been in favour of letting the dead be dead and trying to hold onto the living. This was a waste of time. But Nora and Eleanor sat on the edge of the drop-off looking at the event like it was a matinee. They both wore long flower-print dresses and sat there in the sun drinking lemonade. I would have none of it and went to clean out the cars that my pigeons lived in.

Eventually the chopper wandered off back toward Shearwater and the women came over to where I was shovelling guano.

"Did they find Davey Jones?"

"Nora thought she saw one of the divers come up with a shoe, a rusty pocket watch and a ring," Eleanor told me, somewhat disconcerted, leaving off the rejoinder that, "what Nora sees and what Nora thinks she sees are two different things."

I decided to forget all about it until two weeks later, when a man from Halifax came by with the startling news that my father had been located. The revelation didn't really have any sort of meaning to me at first, but bounced off my head like an India rubber ball.

"Perhaps I should have been more tactful," the man added almost immediately. "I didn't mean to imply that your father is still alive." This was no surprise to me at all. Had he been living, he would have found his way back to the Shore. Nobody leaves this place and stays alive without coming back.

My guest held out the watch and the ring. Both had been polished up as if they were to be resold, good as new. Then, as I looked back at his face, I detected a look of something. . . satisfaction. "Our people are very good in restoration. I asked them to take special care since there is such a wonderful story behind all this. They tell me that, with a bit more attention, they might even be able to get the watch ticking again." Then he couldn't seem to stop himself from smiling.

The bastard, I thought. I slammed the door closed in his face and stood behind it, urging myself into believing that there was something very important in the rivers of the wood grain—the dry, taut boards with their graceful, distinct highways that ran top to bottom. The man knocked on the door a second time. I opened it, motioned for him to come in. He bowed his head and entered.

Tom Burchell worked for the Provincial Archives in Halifax. "You can call me by my Christian name," he said as I poured him a cup of boiling hot tea and the steam fogged up his rimless glasses. "Your father has proven to be quite a fascinating subject for investigation. He was an amazing character from what I can piece together. You probably can't appreciate the complexity of researching a story such as his."

I had lost my father in my own memory now for so many years that it shocked me for him to suddenly appear in my imagination again, a big hulking man with a solid hand, leading me down to the waterfront in Halifax, carrying me up Portland Street in Dartmouth and setting me in a wagon. And then simply his hard, rough cheek grinding my face as he was about to leave for the first of so many times in my life. I suddenly realized what sort of driving force had existed in him. It was here inside of me too, but different; his restlessness had translated itself into a desire to hold things together, to hold on. I felt like an electromagnet responsible for holding the entire world together. If I let go, it would all be over. I was holding out against the sea, holding out against decay, patching up ancient barns, forever fixing an old house, trying to keep my ancient automobiles from cracking into rust and sliding back to soil. Holding out against time. Holding fast onto Eleanor and holding inside an image of my father who I had believed, against logic, would somehow appear again even though he would have been over ninety.

"These were your father's," Burchell said, placing the ring and watch on the table. "You'll want to know what we found out." It wasn't a question.

"First, let me make myself credible," Burchell stated with a calm, intent look on his face. "I'm an archivist by profession. Are you familiar with the nature of my work?" I nodded.

"History, for the most part, remains unwritten. It's rather incredible how much of it we let slip away. I retrieve what I can of it. One collects and catalogues details until something takes shape. I started out in law—criminal law, then international law. It took me to Nuremburg where I did legwork for some of the finest researchers after the war. But I began to find it more challenging to piece together stories of those long since dead rather than the recently murdered. I must admit, I would get carried away. Before I settled here, I even found myself studying the bones of Egyptian mummies, trying to determine what they died from, if in fact they were murdered and why. But such work is, ultimately, all rather academic now, isn't it?

"When they brought me here to your province, I thought of how much had already been lost: the Acadians, the fishing communities, the Native way of life even. So much has been erased that it would take more than one man to piece together

history here. Believe me, very little has really been done. But
I've given up on the big picture. I settle for the reconstruction
of one individual life at a time. If that life interests me."

There was that smile again. What was it? A cocky self–
assurance? I almost felt that he was mocking me with his air
of self-importance.

"Now, your father had quite a fascinating life."

"You told me that." He clearly loved the little drama and
didn't mind what it was costing me. Decades had passed, I had
no reason to fill in the years in minutes.

"I'll get to the point, the part of his life you don't know about,
then run along. If you have any questions, feel free to call . . ."
He placed one more item on the table, some sort of metal
identification strip made of brass, polished to a brittle shine.
There was a long string of numbers and a swastika. "Don't be
alarmed. It's from an aircraft your father stole. Apparently he
learned to fly it quite well.

"The twin-engine plane came from Holland, that we know.
The Germans had moved in while your father was in an
asylum. I even found the cause of his admission. He had been
found in a fishing boat with a dead motor on the North Sea
where he had been drifting for many days, weeks perhaps. It's
a touching story. The Dutch heard him ranting and raving in
such an odd accent that they put him away for the time being
until somebody could figure out who he was. Only the
Germans came and disrupted, shall we say, the normalcy of
society. I suppose he simply escaped the hospital and then
stole the plane. Clearly he had learned something about
airplanes before his arrival in Holland. The Nazis reported
that someone had stolen from their own base one of the most
ancient, least dependable craft on the lot. I had to dig deep
to find that record, believe me. Not many cared about the loss
of a mere training craft when all around them, the war was
caving in.

"I can only fill in the empty spaces, but my next piece of
concrete evidence is that the plane touched down about a
month later in St. John's, Newfoundland, where your father

made quite a splash in the papers. Everyone was sure he was a Gestapo spy. The Newfoundlanders had been so eager to see the war come close to home that everyone wanted to believe that your father was a spy, but nobody knew why he would have arrived in such a desperate state at such great personal risk, in broad daylight. The plane was impounded and he was closely scrutinized, fed well and eventually written up as a hoax. Apparently he could no longer speak properly—damage to the vocal cords, perhaps from his former stay at sea without liquids; I'm just guessing here. But it confused the issue. They, too, thought him a lunatic. You'll pardon my expression.

"But your father had a certain drive, shall we say. He commandeered the plane again and, in a heavy fog, found his way back here. He might even have been trying to ditch the plane on purpose out there. But he didn't get out. We're all sorry. This was all quite some time ago that this happened, of course."

I couldn't say a word. My ears rang as blood pumped inside my head, my heart having swelled up to fill my chest. I knew I hadn't even been here when the plane went down. I was in Halifax, chopping cod, falling in love with Eleanor, but after that, we moved out to this place. What had drawn us to this spot?

Burchell poured himself more of the hot, bitter tea, drained his cup and stood up. "If you want me, I'll be at this number on the card. He must've had quite a story, your father. Don't quote me on the rest, since it remains pure speculation and I consider myself a man of facts, but, my guess is simply this. After getting away from the Nazis, your father must have flown north around the east coast of England, up to the Orkneys, say, refuelling God knows how many times, then across to Iceland, Greenland maybe, then down to Newfoundland. Nice trick in a rig like that but luck was with him. Until the end, of course. Luck does always run out, though, you know."

* * *

"You should be eating more," Nora told me as I put my shirt back on over my burnt shoulders. I felt like a living flame and Nora could see right into the heart of it.

"Don't worry. You won't be going to hell. When you die, the sky will open up like a sliced pie and a hand will pull you up feet first. You'll get yourself a job teaching angels to step dance and that will be that."

"That's good news."

"It's been going like that for me these days. My programmer seems to be tuning me into different stations." I was surprised how the twentieth century had even caught up to Nora. Her guides had become programmers. "Like that kid over there." Nora had discovered the silent Kelly who had walked herself over to the chesterfield and lay down, falling asleep instantly. Her breathing filled the hollow room with such warmth. I was almost afraid to name the intoxicating substance that poured in on me from my past, my future, my supremely conscious present. Nora was reading her as she slept. "It's not often I look at a young woman and see seven beautiful children smiling from her belly. Kids don't want a lot of kids these days. But look at her. Seven squirmy little spirits locked up in her, waiting for the right time. Pity it always takes a man to unlock the womb."

Nora got up to go. "I know you don't need the warning, Jonas, but I suggest you keep your keys to yourself." Nora had put on her rimless glasses for the first time since she arrived. It made her look like a schoolteacher we both had once way back there at the Green Hill School. Nora claimed that putting them on stopped the visions. "Push reality up sharper into anybody's face and it'll frig up reception on all the other channels. Sometimes, a body wants that." I got up to see Nora to the door. She turned to me abruptly and gave me a hug. Two ancient bags of bones crushed against each other on a summer afternoon. "Had I picked you instead of that stupid fisherman to chase, I never would have let you go." She walked out the door and I was left standing alone on a worn-down hardwood floor listening to Kelly breathe. Inside, I filled up with a bright light that wanted to burst out of my rib cage. Through the screen door, I saw Nora, forty years younger, walking in a long green dress through the field of browning timothy. She was walking off toward the sloping crest of the drumlin where sky and earth bit hard together in the clean absolute geometry of summer.

Sitting on the floor beside Kelly, I cupped her long soft hair into my hand and pushed it up to my face, then I brushed my cheek against hers and found that room in Halifax, found Eleanor sleeping beside me, found in that brief thirty-second lifetime everything I needed. And then the very floorboards beneath me that I had nailed tight into their beams so many years ago pulled me down into a warm well of blackness.

I must have slept like that right there for a full twenty hours because the next morning when Nora came back, again wearing her glasses to subdue the visions and worrying over my morality, she was surprised at what she saw. What Nora thought she saw was the frail carcass of a dead man crumpled up on the floorboards of my house. But she was wrong. And when she took off her glasses, she saw that he was the most permanently alive person she had ever come across in her wanderings through several planes of existence.

She went out, gathered a dozen pigeon eggs and cooked them up as a breakfast for me. She read the note from Kelly on the back of the drawing left on the table and wasn't going to let me read it until later. When the seed of consciousness finally took root and broke the soil of sleep, I sat up. What I thought I saw was Nora sitting on a kitchen chair stark naked and radiant, the most beautiful old bag of bones I had ever set eyes upon.

_____**Wings**

The first time I saw Joe Allen Joe was when he appeared at the doorway of Margaret's house. It was during that brief, unsettling phase after my mother had died yet before my father disappeared into the world. Joe Allen snared rabbits in the winter and would go door to door selling them for almost nothing. I always thought it unfair to see even a rabbit's life cut short by snaring wire and to have its carcass sold for less than the cost of cigarettes. But rabbits were considered good food in these parts and for Joe Allen Joe, the only living remnant of the Micmacs in this area, it was a living.

To my father, who had a genuine curiosity in things, Joe Allen was a real find. He bought eight rabbits from the Indian and told him to sit down and talk. Joe Allen would probably have been no more than a teenager then but, to me, he loomed in the doorway like a giant. His hands were stained with the dried blood of rabbits and his hair was dramatically long. I had never seen a man with such profuse black hair dangling about his shoulders. It was tied at the base of his neck into a knot.

After he was seated at Margaret's table, my father challenged him to arm wrestle. This must have been some reaction of his from seeing pictures in books or from the early silent films where Indians were portrayed as savages whose lives depended on challenges of physical strength.

It was soon after that when my father disappeared and I drifted into my own private life of growing up on the shore without a family. I became interested in all the other loners I could track down. I asked people about Joe Allen Joe, but it was as if he had sprung up from the earth of its own accord. He had, no doubt, come from further down the Eastern Shore but no one knew exactly where. Most people just called him the Indian and there was a certain way that the words were said that made you feel there was always some unsaid joke shared by anyone who called him that. I grew curious as to where he lived and for a while was under the impression that Joe simply lived inside a tent of animal skins as my school textbook suggested.

I put the question to Margaret who had no answer, the information not being her business, as she would say. So I carried the concern down to the wharf and asked Edgar MacBride who was hacking off cod heads amidst the constabulary of herring gulls. "What? You don't know about Big Chief Crooked Castle?" he asked. "Him live in home nailed to the trees, sleep with dead rabbits and wild animals." The men laughed, the gulls laughed and when I went back to try again for some answer from Margaret, I prodded her with what I had been told.

"He bought a piece of land from the county at a tax sale. A piece of scrub spruce out on the other side of the lake. They say he paid for it with a hundred rabbit pelts. The land was going for twenty dollars, back taxes. No one wanted it. So the county sheriff took the pelts, I guess, and gave Joe Allen the land. He started to build a house out of salvaged mill scraps nailed onto the trees. Not a right angle in the place, they say.

He nailed all his walls to the trees so that it's shaped like something out of a jigsaw puzzle and that's where he lives. But he don't bother nobody and mostly, nobody bothers him."

I tried to convince John Kincaid to walk up the far side of the lake with me one winter but he couldn't, because of the impracticality of it, Kincaid being a young man of profit motivation by that time. So I set off across the frozen lake by myself on one of those days in March when the winter retreats back into its cave and you're left with confusing summery warmth that turns the roads to rubber and melts clear diamond ice into a milky sponge, still thick enough to support weight but not to be fully trusted. At night the cold from beneath would try to glaze the surface back to glass, but then by late morning the puddles sprang up and a thin, slippery veneer glossed over the white ice below.

I had on nothing but two sweaters as I slouched across the mile or so of frozen lake. A thick fog had settled over the whole area before I reached mid-ice and it was like I was walking in a dream. The world was without colour or sound save the slapping of my boots through the water. When I stopped for an instant to test my bearings, a raven flew past me at eye level, close enough for me to see the reptile shank of its legs pulled back in flight. One black eye seemed to bore right through me and left a chill in my bones. The sound of the wings cutting the air was like the whoosh of a sword slashing out in a fight. But I don't think the raven gave in to the fact that I was present. Birds, too, are perhaps confronted by hallucinations and for him, I was just another frightening, inexplicable form rearing up out of the fog.

I walked on for what must have been an hour and then resigned myself to the fact that I must be completely lost; maybe I had turned up the lake instead of across, in which case, I might go on like this for days, heading thirty miles or more inland. Or if I was headed south, I might find this step or the next without ice beneath the deepening water on the surface. My feet would find the saltier taste of the inlet at the foot of Rigger's Lake and I would feel the grip of cold sea pulling at my helpless legs.

I closed my eyes and walked. The winter warmth made everything seem impossible, unreal, the earthbound cloud intoxicated me with its damp warmth and I felt strangely pleased to have found a manifestation of my inner isolation and loneliness now tangible and all around me as if I had conspired it into being. The loss of my mother, the absence of my father. Only John Kincaid had given me a stable sense of who I was. But here I was alone, slushing through limbo and pleased to be forever lost. I would count the steps and not look. If I could go a full one hundred strides and not open my eyes or drown or fall off the face of the earth, it would be settled, a bargain would be hammered out with the Almighty and He would concede that I was invulnerable and capable of living forever. By thirty paces my face was twitching with a sort of pleasurable terror. By fifty I was gaining confidence and by eighty (giddy with the notion that I would get my way and already wanting to renegotiate the terms) I wanted more than mere immortality. I wanted the return of my mother from the dead and my father from the living.

When I had shouted out "ninety-nine," triumphantly ready for my return to vision, a voice spoke out of the cloud, "You sure picked some funny place to practise arithmetic." I opened my eyes and looked down at my feet. Before me was a round hole through the ice measuring four feet across. The water floated a random geometry of ice chunks and a fishing line descended into the lake beneath. Joe Allen sat on a rough wooden bench a few feet in front of me wearing a short-sleeved shirt and a dreamy look on his face. His hair was loose and fell about his shoulders like the shiny black wing of the lost raven.

"You like smelts? Try one, maybe. Some people don't mind 'em raw and frozen."

I looked at the pile of bug-eyed little fish, a few flopping in the puddles, a few slipping over into death with crooked smiles and angled backs. "No thanks."

"Me neither. White people think Indians eat anything raw. My father did, but not me. Gives you bad breath."

"How do you know where to fish?"

Joe Allen laughed but it was a different sort of laugh than anything I knew of. When you live that much alone, you start to do things differently, I figured. "I use my ears," was his answer.

"You listen?"

"I put down a piece of leather on the ice, put my ear to it and listen. The currents tease me, the ice has things to say. But the fish speak too. Sometimes they fool me. I'm not always right. That's the game. You know how many languages there are in the world? Everything that *is* has a language. Fish, rabbits, trees, ice. You hear them noises when it cracks? The ice speaks to itself. It's dreaming. It dreams itself back to water each spring. I know, I've seen it do that."

Then a strange thing happened. Joe Allen pulled up his line with a hooked fish on it and set it down. Then suddenly another smelt jumped right out the hole beside it and slapped itself down on the ice.

"You made that happen?"

"No. That one just wanted to know what was on the other side of the ice."

"He wanted to die?"

"He just wanted to know what was on the other side of the ice. Like you might want to know what's on the other side of the sky. Doesn't mean you want to be dead." Joe dipped both his hands in the icy water, then picked up the fish and gently eased it back into the cold water, lowering his hand slowly and watching the fish drift below into a current.

"Some day, someone might do the same for me. I always wanted to know what was on the other side from being born. What I was before my mother and father made me. But I sure don't want to die finding out."

"I heard your mother and father are dead."

"Gone."

"How?"

"Indians are different from you. We live and die in our own ways. One day they realized they had no place left that was their own and they could not live with that. My father had lived his life inside his father's world and his father's world was no longer there. You might not understand."

"I think I do." Now that I had stopped walking, the dampness was settling back into my bones. I started to dance around in a shuffle the way I had learned to do when I was getting really chilled. Margaret called it my jig. Joe looked at me with a surprising anger and stood bolt upright, grabbing both my wrists. He looked hard into my face with brooding black eyes and our breath assembled in a quiet cloud before us. I stopped moving and he sat back down, still looking at me with an immobilizing stare. I was afraid to move and felt the soles of my boots freezing into place.

In a minute I saw the wraiths of two men with guns passing behind Joe, not more than fifty feet away. They were coughing and spitting the way that men on the shore do and in a second they were lost from sight. Two old scoundrels from the inlet, no doubt, going up the lake to shoot the geese who would be settled on a remote stretch of lake, grounded by the fog and totally helpless against a spray of lead shot that would kill a dozen for each shell thumbed into the barrel. I had always thought it grossly unfair to shoot geese and ducks that way. Sometimes, so many were shot that they'd have to leave half of them to rot on the ice but I'd seen how they couldn't quit once the deed was started. The birds who got away flew blindly into the curtained sky and often became so disoriented before they could get high out of the fog that they were snared by trees, breaking wings. Then they scuttled around the forest until a fox or a dog could have at them.

"Congratulations," Joe said, after a while, "you are now invisible."

"Are you afraid of them?"

Joe shook his head.

"What would they have done if we were not invisible?"

"Laughed." Joe Allen began to gather his catch into a burlap bag. He pushed a large slab of ice back into the hole where it fit like a hatch door. Then he gently brushed the surface around where we stood until there was a thin, even film of water that would freeze over in the night. "It was good of the lake to let me borrow this place. Now I go. Do you know your way back?"

I told him that I didn't. Some ways off I heard the first blasts from the shotguns. The sound could have come from anywhere. Then the squawking of geese ringing in the air. More shots. More desperate geese, natives of Labrador, heading home and caught on an unforgiving lake in Nova Scotia. When I looked around me Joe Allen was gone without a trace. I was completely alone in some alien place on the other side of living. But I was not dead.

* * *

The cold fog hugged the land like a thick blanket for what must have been months and I felt sure that Joe Allen had been responsible for it. He was trying to hold onto his invisibility for as long as he could, although I never dared to suggest that to any of the men at the wharf. You could tell that the fog made them all jumpy through the spring, if that's the season it was. The ice was gone from the lakes and harbours before March was out, but none had decided to leave the safety of the harbour until the sun cracked through enough to reassure them that they wouldn't fall off the edge of the earth. The war in Europe had ended but here it seemed like it had never happened. When you can barely see your hand in front of your face, it's hard to believe in anything a few thousand miles away—especially people killing each other over the ownership of land or the naming of a country. Even though all of the men knew my father in one way or another, none would say a word about him or ask me if I had any news. When someone left the shore, often it was like he had left the world for good.

I hadn't forgotten about Joe Allen but had done some reading about the Indians. The Beothuk, the Malecite, the giant Dorsets and the Micmac. The Beothuk were gone from

Newfoundland where they had once lived out simple lives along the harsh coast. When the English came the Beothuk hid themselves away, almost starving whole communities to death rather than feel the wrath of the white savages. But they were soon hunted down and killed or died off from the new diseases. They were all gone except for a few stray survivors, literally the last of their race who would soon be gone. I wondered what it would be like to be the last of something. Then I realized that with my mother gone, and my father away somewhere maybe forever, I was myself the last of my family. But I was planning on being around for a long time.

The Micmac were in no immediate danger of extinction, but they once had the whole of Nova Scotia to themselves. Until we intruded. They had sided with the French and fought the English but not with any great conviction. There was great anger in them from having been interrupted in their annual migration from coast to inland and back. They thought the English were fools for wanting to live the year out along the coast without retreating inland during the stormy winters. But the English were stupid that way.

* * *

I didn't mind helping Garnie Bruce mend his nets when I could and it gave me a good excuse to sit around and listen to the men talk. I loved the half-rotted little shacks that they used for their fishing business. Many of the men slept there as often as they could even though they had better homes nearby and each shack had been constructed in a hasty, haphazard manner that made it look like they would be blown away during a mild gale. Garnie had a hole in the floor of his shack so that he could spit out tobacco juice. His teeth were a corroded black and brown configuration that, when he smiled, made him look like he possessed his own private cave of horrors. He claimed his wife never kissed him anymore since he lost most of his uppers.

"But frig it," he would say. "What can a man do?" Garnie would pee through the same hole in the floor and it went down into the harbour, the spit, the pee, all the garbage anybody could haul, anything rotten or useless. Dumped off the dock. Then in the summer, like other boys, I'd sit there with a pole over the edge and catch mackerel and sea perch and take them home to Margaret to cook. She always thought that fish caught by the wharf tasted "sweeter" than anything landed at sea.

Garnie had a bent frame, a crooked man from top to bottom, all angles, cheekbones, knees and shoulder blades that were so sharp they would cut through his clothes, never to be repaired. He never once asked me a question about myself or even said hello or thanked me for my net work. He just talked my ear off about anything that came into his head, mostly his theories about how the world worked, then he'd pee or spit down his hole in the floor and study it for a minute before going back to lecturing. I could come and go as I pleased. He would stop talking after I left but he never said goodbye. Still, it was a good place to learn something about what was going on in the world.

"You gots to understand, that it's the bastards always come out on top. Thieves and liars usually do the best. After that, the suckholes, then maybe comes your killers and murderers, but they only kill 'cause they're too damn stupid to steal well. The peoples that work always come out on the bottom. Sometimes, if you're damn good at being plain lazy, you can convince the thieves that you're on their side and get by that way. I don't mind the liars and thieves really. It's the suckholes that get my goat." Garnie's hierarchy was, to his way of thinking, absolute. Since he considered himself one of the few people in the world who did any honest labour, and as far as I could tell there were maybe only a few thousand of his minority in the whole world, he figured he was forever on the bottom.

"Take Selwyn Rigger for example now, would ya? Selwyn gets himself a great-great-grandfather first off who pleads he's a bloody Loyalist. That is, he made a killing for the Brits selling tea and rum in the Boston States until the boys get a little tinkered off about the price of a little refreshment. They tell old Tory Rigger to cut it down to somethin' fair or else, but the old fart don't give in . . . He's got the fartin' King's army behind him and he keeps pushin' up the prices till the boys in the colony run him out of town. Only when he marches back in, he's got the army with him firing bullets.

"So in the end, he gets the old heave-ho when the Yanks get their revolution going, and he sails up to Halifax where they treat the old thief like a hero. The King, you remember the one who used to froth at the mouth and puff himself up red in the face when he gave speeches, he gave Rigger a couple of ships and told him to go ram hell out of the American boats. Shit, Rigger sat on his butt in Halifax while his privateers did the dirties for him. But in the end, after they'd lost the war, the government here give him half of bloody Halifax County.

"Only, a couple of generations later, Selwyn loses most of it to taxes. Proves my point about suckholes not doing nearly as well as outright thieves. To add insult to injury, the Indian ups and buys a hundred acres on Rigger's Lake, just south of where Selwyn's holed up, buys it up with pelts for frig's sake. Nobody but an Indian could get away with buying frig-all with pelts these days, but the Indian does. Right now, Selwyn's trying to get his land back. I don't think the Indian knows it. But Selwyn claims that it ain't right for a heathen to get land that once belonged to a Christian. He has the church behind him. Religion is always good for making a mountain out of a mole's hair for the sake of giving somebody a hard time. Usually, it's only religion and money that get people killed. People say it's women too, but I don't think women are up there with religion and money. Selwyn, sweet Jesus, he still owns only twenty thousand acres even after losing most of it. County give half of it back because his grandfather was such a good Loyalist. And a Christian. But Rigger don't like the idea of no Indian living on what's *rightfully* his." Garnie got up to pee again. Three times on the hour was his habit. And he'd spit twenty-five times for every pee. If I owned a watch I could have set it by his schedule. Nothing seemed to change it. Then he sat back down and stared at the wall opposite him. That's the way he usually spoke, staring past me at a wood plank wall with the studs exposed and nothing on the inside but the backside of the outer wall.

"Selwyn'll win, too. I don't know where Indians fit in line. I don't think they were meant to. That's why we took over to begin with. To give the liars and thieves a fairer chance. Now I'm kind of fond of the notion of privateers myself, so I don't have nothing on them. Like I say, I can even tolerate a good thief or an outright liar because they don't make any bones about who they are and everyone knows it. But I don't like no suckhole and that's our boy Selwyn. And the Indian don't stand a chance."

* * *

I couldn't help but wonder if Joe Allen knew what was up. I had heard about Selwyn before, met him once, and never forgot the smell. He was a bulky six foot, and wore old suits around even though he lived way up in the woods on Rigger's Lake, named after his family. Some jokingly called him the mayor of Rigger's Lake, though there was never really a town there. Selwyn had once shown up at Margaret's on a Sunday afternoon asking my father to invest some money in a business proposition he had going. He was starting up a mail-order house for salves and ointments. Other kinds of cures too. All he wanted was a little "spending money for advertisement." Capital is what he needed. My father didn't go for it, of course, but Kincaid's old man did, lost a hundred dollars and all he had to show for it in the end was a case of something that smelled like pickle juice that was supposed to remove corns and warts.

Selwyn never married. According to Garnie, it was because of a "women's disease" he had picked up from sleeping with unsavoury ladies. But he had a man who worked for him— chopped wood, rowed him back and forth across the lake and such. Selwyn was the only man on the shore I ever knew who didn't row his own boat. And the only man I ever knew who smelled like sour milk twenty-four hours a day. Maybe it had something to do with his disease. Although there had once been a dozen families of Riggers on Rigger's Lake, Selwyn was the only one left and he wanted the lake and the land that was "rightfully" his back in his own Christian hands.

The day after hearing Garnie's story, I skipped net mending and went looking for Joe Allen. I walked up the east side of the lake since the ice was well gone. The fog hadn't fully lifted so it was a bit hard finding my way. I had been told that there had been summers in the past when the fog had stayed thick as couch grass all summer and I didn't know if Joe Allen could hold out that long.

I walked maybe five miles up along the shoreline to where I thought I had encountered Joe a month or so back on the ice and I wondered how I was supposed to find the man who claimed to be invisible. I would never have found his house, but there he was sitting at the edge of Rigger's Lake on a huge boulder that put him up almost as high as the tops of the spruce trees.

He saw me first. "You have very good eyes for a boy. Or maybe my magic is wearing off. If I'm not careful, I'll not be able to hold onto this cloud much longer." He pointed up into the air.

"You made the fog?"

"No, of course not. I just borrowed it. I like the way it makes me feel inside. But now my birds want their sky back. So I should let it go."

I didn't believe him, of course, but I liked the way he said it. And somehow I wasn't expecting his English to be so good.

"What birds?"

"Come. I'll show you. Your eyes are good, but you would never find my house."

He led me down a path that was not a path into the spruce tent of the forest, through gnarly undergrowth and rocks that stood out like teeth on the forest floor. He had a way of dod-ging around obstacles and ducking under overhanging branches that I tried to copy, only to get myself tangled again and again in tree branches that seemed to reach out and grab.

"Be more polite," Joe said to the trees, then turned to me. "They're just not used to you. You'll have to forgive them."

After that, it did seem that they let up. I lost Joe once in one of those stretches where young spruce trees grow in thick like weeds and crowd out everything, tall and spindly and wedged against each other, killing each other off with their advance toward light. Then just as quickly, he was behind me. "They have no manners," he said about the young trees.

And then we were there, at the home of Big Chief Crooked Castle. It was very much like as they had described it. All angles and odd shapes, wood lashed, not nailed, to a variety of older spruce trees that had grown here and there, making the rough-cut boards shift to crazy angles. I had never seen anything like it. It had a roof of loose boards and spruce boughs with a hole in the middle for smoke to sift out. "The trees don't mind it this way at all," he said.

"We are good neighbours. But first the birds." I followed him along a path around the house to another small building, a tree house again, but this one off the ground. A rope ladder led up into it and I followed him inside.

"Pigeons?" I asked, somewhat baffled.

"Carrier pigeons. Look how big they are. And beautiful. And almost all gone from the face of the earth."

"I don't get it."

"Neither do they. Hunters come and kill them all. No one thought they would ever end so they just kept shooting. Now they are all gone. Except for these. Six male, six female. They want me to lift the fog. Tomorrow, I promise."

The pigeons cooed and paced about, larger and louder than any I had ever seen in Halifax. Brown, mottled, some with piercing blue-green or brown-red eyes. There were three open windows. Clearly they were free to come and go as they pleased.

"I came to tell you about Selwyn Rigger," I told Joe.

"Please, not here. They shouldn't know." Then he was out and down the rope ladder. I followed him into his house. From the inside, I could see that it was actually quite tight,

everything fit perfectly together, yet there was little of anything at a right angle, or cut square. There was furniture, all
made from rough sawed boards and one wall was full of books.
Shelves top to bottom held hundreds of volumes, more than
I had ever seen.

"You read a lot."

"The Indian reads quite well. Most of these books were given
to me. I feed the poorer ones to Glooscap." Glooscap
presented himself presently, a porcupine with a mild disposi-
tion. He was chewing off the binding of a book called *Ten
Nights in a Bar Room* by T. S. Arthur.

Joe Allen Joe sat down at a table shaped like the back of a
whale. It wasn't flat on top at all. His seat was a smoothed stone,
mushroom-shaped and of one piece. "You can speak in front
of Glooscap, he knows all about Selwyn and so do I. Selwyn is
one of the few people who can see me. It's because he hates
me so much. He thinks I stole his land. Sometimes hate gives
invisible people shape. Even the Indian. Selwyn comes with
his man, Keesy. First he came with jugs of rum. It was very bad
but very good and I drank it all. But it didn't kill me. It was
supposed to. Then he sent Keesy down with a gun and poor
Keesy hid all day outside waiting for me. I played a game on
him and Death together. I sneaked out into the woods like a
good Indian then let Keesy and Death follow until we were far
away. The carriers stayed above me to let me know how I was
doing. I left Keesy and his partner very lost. When I went back
to find Keesy several days later, using the carriers to tell me
his whereabouts, he was very mad. Angry men make me truly
sad. He tried to shoot me with his gun, but it wouldn't work
because of the rain which had made it rusty. See, I have friends
everywhere. I had to take him back to Selwyn before he lost
his mind. Some white men are not so good with their minds.
So now Selwyn wants to get rid of me again. How this time?"

I explained about the government, that Rigger had gone to
court and the law had agreed he had a right to his property
back, on the grounds that since Joe Allen Joe was not a
Christian, he was not by definition of the law a human being

and therefore his purchase of the land with animal skins was
not legitimate. What Selwyn had actually argued was that "an
animal can't own land, can he?" But I didn't repeat that part.

"But I am a very religious man. Ask the trees."

He was certainly that. But I did not know if he had the power
to overcome the law. And I wanted to be sure that Joe Allen
would be around for a long time. His sense of quiet, calm
reserve was nothing I had encountered in the men from the
docks and I would like to have learned his trick.

"I have made peace with Death. I don't think Selwyn can use
it against me. It worked against my father, but not me."

I wanted to try to explain that the law and government could
be worse than death. I tried my best but stumbled over the
words. Joe Allen tried to follow my stuttering. He had strong
dark eyes and sat bolt upright with Glooscap at his feet
nibbling the first chapter of his book.

"He'll win, you know. I've seen him around people." I'm
afraid I had succumbed to Garnie's understanding of the
hierarchy of the world. Selwyn was not a good liar and was too
stupid to be a good thief, but he was an excellent suckhole.
Everyone knew that.

Joe Allen looked puzzled. He gathered his long hair into his
palm and unbraided it. It was a soft, rich black that spilled
down to his chest. "What should I do then? You obviously came
here to save me. That's why I was not invisible to you. Love
and hate both work."

I was embarrassed by what he said. I didn't know about the
love part, but I didn't like the thought of him getting kicked
off the land and losing his crooked castle.

"Go ahead," he said, "tell me what I should do."

"Become a Christian."

"And become a human being?" I couldn't tell if he took me
seriously or thought it a joke.

"Just get baptised."

"Hmm. There are so many gods, it would be hard to pick
just one."

* * *

So I went ahead and picked one for him. Me, a runt of a kid, selecting a god for this man of spirit. I would take him out to Muriel and her Baptist who had professed to be a legitimate minister. Joe liked the thought of a trek out to Penchant Point but worried over the dunking in the ocean. "My guess is they'll want to do it in the sea. I don't think they would settle for any smaller piece of water," I explained.

"This could be a problem. I've made many bargains with the lake but the sea is harder to make terms with. She might not want to give me back."

"It's only for a few seconds," I assured him, but what did I know of Baptists? I knew Muriel was probably nothing short of crazy, but she hadn't yet done away with her half-black, half-white husband who had come to save the coast and settled for saving grace with Muriel on an icy finger of land too far into the reach of the sea for its own good. I would take Garnie Bruce just in case. But also because I needed a witness.

* * *

"Fried spit, what are you talking about, boy?" I think it was the first time Garnie ever addressed me directly. I had never heard that phrase before. But Garnie's understanding of the contrary powers of the natural world were no match for the Indian.

"Look, Garnie, the fog is gonna lift."

"Liftin' Jesus, it's not gonna lift. I understand fog like this and it's settled here for a good two months. You're too young to understand how these things work. It's trying to starve us to death. So I ain't taking my boat all the way out to crazy-as-an-eel Muriel and her great grey husband and I sure as sand ain't gonna walk out to that God-forsaken place."

Garnie never believed it possible for himself to be wrong about things, and therefore, was willing to make a bet. So I tempted him. "If the fog doesn't lift by tomorrow, I'll fix the rest of your nets by myself, save you some work. But if it does lift by tomorrow you'll take us out to Penchant Point and be a witness for the baptising."

Garnie got up to pee through the hole in the floor of his shed, a long steady stream that echoed beneath the floor as it splashed into the water below. "Well, you better do a friggin' good job on the nets, boy. You got a deal."

So the fog lifted just as Joe had predicted and everybody went fishing except for Garnie who found an Indian, a smug boy and a pair of carrier pigeons waiting for a ride out to Penchant Point. Garnie never looked once at the Indian. He just kept staring at the jagged shoreline of the peninsula. "I've never knowed one person who lived out here on this slab of rock who wasn't stupid or crazy," he pontificated. "Crazy people lead interesting lives, I'll grant them that, but stupid people live to be ninety years old, every one of 'em. If I was hiring men, I'd hire ten dumb clucks before I took on one crazy bugger, that's for sure. Stupid people know how to work. They're just not too smart. Crazy people just keep getting crazier. They have to put a lot of energy into it. Sometimes you have a crazy person who's good at lying and thieving. Then you have a problem. Get one into the government, then look out. If I had my druthers, I'd only elect stupid people. Then we'd see."

Garnie was still a little sore about losing the gamble. First time he was ever wrong in his whole life, he told the Indian. Joe was holding a pair of his carrier pigeons, one in each hand. "They need the flying after all the low clouds." They seemed perfectly content to be held by Joe.

Garnie didn't like the idea of having birds on a boat. When asked why not, he just said, "Well, there's flyin' and there's floatin'. Birds don't belong on a boat." But he was just sore about being wrong. Other than the pigeons, he didn't really acknowledge that an Indian was on his boat. He didn't really let on that he noticed Joe at all. I was beginning to think that *existential* maybe the Indian was invisible.

We were near the farthest tip of the peninsula when we spotted Muriel and her Baptist standing like two stone monuments at the foot of the cliff beneath their house. They were just staring off at the morning sun. Garnie could pull his boat almost flush up to the black sand beach and we came ashore hardly getting our feet wet. Garnie grumbled a cursory greeting, then wandered off to find a boulder to pee behind. While I was explaining the situation to Muriel and her Baptist, Joe held out his hand. The birds just sat there for a minute on his open palms, finding their legs and remembering their wings. Then they were off flying, circling us round and round in wider arcs. It was maybe the first time I ever really appreciated the grace of flying things.

The Grey Baptist had the same smouldering dark flame in his eyes I had remembered. Muriel looked like she was already living in some world beyond Penchant Point, but both agreed to perform the baptism after Joe explained that he had no problems with believing in the eternal God and the saving power of holy baptism. I pictured him back on the ice, fishing in that winter fog. When I had turned around and found him gone, I had wondered in my fanciful way if he had disappeared down the ice, and did he live beneath the lake? It was never proven to me that Joe was incapable of this. Baptism then should be nothing to him. A little cold sea water on his face.

Muriel and the Baptist, one on each side, led Joe out into the sea until they were all up to their chest in that piercing cold Atlantic bath. As the pigeons circled overhead, Muriel first shouted something to the sky in a language unknown to me. Then the Baptist chanted along in something closer to English but incomprehensible still. Then they locked their arms tight around Joe and pushed his head into the sea. They continued to converse in harsh, pleading voices to the empty sky and an invisible God for a long minute. Joe did not struggle. You could tell they held him down hard, only the tips of his shoulder blades had communion with the air and his long hank of black hair floated out behind him like a snake that lay still on the surface. Garnie and I looked on nervously as the minute stretched out longer. Too long. They were trying to kill him.

And it was my fault. They planned on saving one heathen Indian by washing his soul clean of the earth. I tried to do something but found that I couldn't move.

But then, I realized, they were trying to pull him up, their chanting dying off in the morning air. But it was like he was tied down to something. They pulled and nothing happened. The sea did not want to let him go. A terrifying silence halfway between life and death gripped the whole shoreline. I pleaded with Garnie to help, to do something.

"You can't mess around with crazy people when they're trying to kill each other." He stated that like a fact. He had had experience in that area before. "I'm not stupid, you know."

Finally, my own feet found their legs, found their muscles, and I ran out into a sea that fought back with cold daggers driving hard at my thighs and groin. The first thing I could grab was Joe's hair. I pulled and his head bobbed up. His face had gone blue and I was sure he was dead. The Baptist hefted him up on his shoulders and carried him ashore. They appeared like two giants who had fought some ancient battle. The Baptist stretched Joe out on the shale outcropping. Now he appeared white. Muriel fell down on her knees and began to wail and speak in tongues. Her hands folded into prayer and the Baptist rolled his great dark eyes up toward the empty blue sky. The birds had ceased circling and had flown off inland toward home.

And then, almost before he had taken a single breath of air, Joe Allen Joe opened his eyes and stared at the late morning sun with a calm, broad smile. If his face expressed any stronger emotion it could only be described as genuine surprise.

"I was afraid she might not want to let me go." He didn't mean Muriel. "Like I said, lakes are one thing, but the sea is something else."

Garnie was hovering near now, more interested in life than death. "You're damn straight there, Indian." Joe was no longer invisible to him.

"Praise the Lord," Muriel shouted.

"Praise Jesus," the Grey Baptist thundered.

"It was you who brought me back," Joe said to me, coughing now and vomiting something into the sand.

* * *

When Selwyn Rigger called the Indian before the travelling judge who had set up court in the schoolhouse on a Saturday afternoon, he hadn't heard the story about the baptism. Garnie hadn't told anybody up to that point, abiding by my request. "Don't fret. I won't say spit," he assured me.

The Grey Baptist had even written off to his home office for an official paper decreeing Joe's baptism. The Baptist had been truly ordained, after all. So when the travelling judge arrived he had already been steeped in the nature of the problem by his cronies back in Halifax, and was ready and willing to decree Rigger the rightful owner of the tax-lost land. He didn't know what to make of the new evidence, the baptism certificate, the announcement on the part of Garnie, redfaced with embarrassment, that yes, he had been at the baptism. The judge looked up then at Joe for the first time, amazed that the Indian's face was so peaceful, proud and like something that had been chipped from stone. The judge said simply, "I rule in favour of Joe Allen Joe."

"Does this mean I am a human being?" Joe asked the judge.

"Suffice it to say, you own the land," the judge answered, not wanting the law to be perverted too far toward justice in one day.

"I thank you, sir," was all Joe said as he walked out of the schoolroom.

* * *

Eleanor had the opportunity only once to meet Joe Allen Joe. She and I had settled into our final home on the cliffs across the inlet from Penchant. A man arrived at our door on a bright, cold day with a small cage. I truly didn't know who it was. It wasn't the Indian. He wore a three-piece suit, shined black shoes, and wore close-cropped hair with a stylish city hat.

He had walked out of a magazine. Eleanor stood behind me
in the doorway, then put her small warm hands on my
shoulder.

"As far as I know, these are the last of their kind in the world.
They are all male. You must breed them with other birds to
keep their spirit alive, but there will never be a pure race of
them again. You are the man of life. Please, this small favour."

A car in the driveway was blowing its horn. I saw a very
attractive woman at the wheel.

"Joe, I don't believe it."

"Nor should you. The Indian is gone. He lost what he had
to lose. Now he is invisible again." He shook my hand hard
enough that I could feel the bones in his hands leave a lasting
sensation of something powerful in my palm and on my
fingers. The woman in the car blew the horn again. Then Joe
kissed me lightly on the cheek and was gone.

I was stunned. When I turned around and faced my wife, the
pigeons cooing from their cage at my feet, she smiled in a
baffled way. "I'm jealous," she said and hugged me to her.

_____Giving in to the Darkness

Once, when I was a boy I decided to hike inland, to follow
the gaspereau stream to its source, to go deep into the forest
of stunted spruce and pretend I was lost. I walked up along
the quiet shoreline of the inlet until I found the tickling
summer steam draining its way into the deeper waters. I
hovered there for a few minutes waiting for something to
happen. This was a common feeling for me in the dead of
summers. I would wait for something to happen, expecting
any minute that the world would again explode or that the
sun would drop from the sky or that life on earth would simply
cease to be.

The hollowness inside me that day almost insisted that
something must be done to anchor me back into the world of
feeling and meaning. Here there were hardwood trees with
leaves that rattled in the complacent breeze. The stream itself
was a trivial bleeding of clear fluid from a drying forest. I
turned to travel up along the rocks and see where it found its
origins.

Then I was drawn into the life of this stream as it asked me
to dance from rock to rock, to select, to improvise a path, to

establish a rhythm and to feel the frail song of the watercourse inside my blood. I was there, bounding faster, then slower and with each step finding the jagged direction I wanted. A single word was forming inside me . . . the thing I was truly searching for, but I could not bring myself to utter it and the water did not insist. When I came to a small, clear pool, I was panting heavily as if something had in fact breathed life back into me. The dry, cool green bank of star moss insisted I lie down and sink into its softness, so I rested there with my face by the surface of the water. The ripples of the pool were enough to lull me into a trance and I studied my breathing, my own subtle storm of life against the water surface. A skater spider moved against it and toward my face until its eyes were close enough that I felt we were locked in recognition. This is when boys tell themselves that they have the power of gods and want to demonstrate their deity by killing things, but I did none of that.

At length, the water spider lost interest in this god and twitched his legs, sending him away toward objectives of more importance to him. I plunged my face through the mirror surface now and, with my eyes closed, listened to the lap of water against my cheek and jaws. It wasn't cold or unpleasant and the effect was amniotic.

There was a desire to breathe, to suck in the water. I almost believed that gills would appear and take over, that if I held like that for long enough I could become something other than merely human. The life of natural things seemed so much more vigorous and intense than what I was growing to see in the activity of men and women. We dismiss these idle thoughts as we grow older and more practical, but childhood and adolescence are filled with important moments of self–induced hypnosis which shape us more than we would like to believe.

I raised my face again and felt the sun agree with the wetness on my face. Had anyone been watching me, I was certain, they would have thought me to be some weird, slow child who had lost, or never had, a sensible nature. Maybe that was why the forest had called me that day. I was used to the dominance of the sea, of walking its perimeter and hearing its booming throat, of being overwhelmed by its immensity as if it was the very soul of the world. Now I had sought inland refuge and found it; but still there was something else I was working at. My idleness, my desire to walk along trickling brooks was dictated by something deeper. My life would be filled with searches. There would always be a quest and most times I would never know what I was searching for. This would be the way of living. I knew this now and wondered why no one had ever bothered to say it outright to me. The clearcut things of living were easy to understand but the gnarly, confused rhetoric of the imagination, of vague, illusive desire would always be there, too, hammering away inside the blood and we would spend much of our lives trying to ignore it, or pretend that it was not there.

The red squirrels above me argued, laughed, taunted as they did when dogs were nearby. I looked but couldn't see them; they were lost in the rattling leaves, the click of ingrown branches and the dagger of light knifing through the trees. I moved on, persuaded back to the rockdance. Each boulder and stone asked for me to touch down and grace its back. The music was in my head, the lyric in the wind, and the choreography all around. I was asked to close my eyes and feel it, to jump from rock to rock on sound, on touch, on instinct. And I did. It didn't even surprise me that it worked. The stones themselves used gravity to bring each step square upon its back and then some other force sent me away to the next. I felt liberated from the dictatorship of sight that usually harnessed my waking hours. It was closer to sleep, and as easy and gentle.

At that split-second that I felt the freedom the strongest, it seemed as if something had seized my foot and brought me falling forward. I never opened my eyes but felt the stab of bully granite against my forehead, stunning me with the remembrance of pain and the cruel insistence that I was not of that other world. We forget as adults what pain does to a

young mind. Surprise more than anything. Then anger that
the world should ever urge us this way. I lay perfectly still, my
chest humped over another rounded stone and my head
resting now on what I saw to be a kingdom of lichen gripped
on the cold rock.

I tasted the blood first, then watched as it fell into the clear
water, swirling in a red spiral the way a painter might mix
colours of rage and purity. The sight was magnificent enough
to draw away my own pain and pull me back to the inner world
of the gaspereau stream. I simply sat up and laughed, dizzy,
released from my dream, but allowed to hover on the edge of
consciousness and be dazzled again by the ribbons of sunlight,
the chanting of water on loose stones and the new sight of an
otter that had attended my performance. He made his own
graceful exit upstream, seeming to barely touch down on
rocks as he floated through the air up the trail of the stream
bed. Eventually my body decided against further loss of blood
and I raised myself, wobbling in the thick air, and I began to
follow the otter. The lightness in my head was wonderful and
I felt as if I should stumble on in this way forever, missing the
rock that once held my feet but still pleased with the sunlight
and the dream-like qualities of everything. I came upon a
small lake surrounded on three sides by low green hills.
Seagulls bobbed on the blue water, but it was nothing like the
sea.

I broke free of the forest and found myself in a soft, moist
world of sundews, ferns and spongy ground covered in green
mosses. I looked up at the sky and felt a great pain in my head
as I focussed on the sun itself. I closed my eyes and held the
lids together tightly with my fists. The throbbing inside my
skull wanted more space, it wanted to get out and it suddenly
occurred to me that I was about to lose consciousness. I was
certain I was about to die. Dark swirling purple wings folded
up around me and I was pulled into a place soft and warm.

As I fell to the ground again, it seemed to take forever. The
fall was without beginning or end, and I had lost all sense of
up or down. My body dissolved from the ankles up and soon

like Kincaid

there would be nothing left of me but whatever was creating these thoughts. And then that too would be gone. It was simple enough.

Suddenly, my mother was there inside the purple darkness and holding out something, a pillow of green for my head. I wanted her so badly but I was being pulled back to the throbbing pain. I didn't want to lose her again. But as I moved back toward the pain, I could sense her less real than before. So I gave in to the darkness. She was there all around me and I was home again in my bed in Halifax before the explosion that had ended one world for me and sent me into this other life. I thought that she was ready to accept me, that we would be together again. But I was wrong. Not yet, she was telling me. Then she was laughing. She shook her head as if to let me know how foolish I had been.

So I slept on a bed of peat and moss and when my eyes found light again I was looking at the drops of water on the mitts of a sundew flytrap, the red, delicate fibres that gathered light and food and curled tight fists around its sustenance. And there was something more. My eyes were slow to relearn how to focus, to move from one thing up close to the background, or to another subject.

A girl was kneeling before me. Her face was almost without expression, a blank slate to write anything upon. She was watching me breathe, watching me pull oxygen into my lungs as if she had never seen another human do it before. I wondered if other angels had gathered around me as well.

I sat up but could not speak, hoping for her to say something first, but she did not. A snake slid by me on the ground and circled a nearby boulder, then went on. The girl stood up, turned and walked away. I was left on my own again and wasn't ready for the new fear of being alone that settled into my bones and wrapped like barbed wire around my throat making me scream something hoarse and incomprehensible. But the girl did not turn around.

With some difficulty I found my feet, made the world go vertical again and followed her across the floating bog that circled the lake. I called out to her but she didn't turn around. She was a frail girl, my own age perhaps, and she walked in a way I had never seen before, as if her feet put no weight on the surface at all. There was something light and other-worldly about her that did not help convince me that I was still of the same place from whence I had fallen. I was even afraid to catch up to her, to look at her face again, not certain of what I would see—the eyes of the holy or the mask of the dead. The inland world had already proven to be a land of tricksters. And I had been proven wrong. The interior was not a place of safety after all and things were not to be trusted.

She led me to a small, perfectly square tarpaper shack where she sat down outside on a three-legged stool carved from a tree stump. She was not surprised that I had followed her and she offered me something to drink from a pitcher. Goat's milk. The sour, acidic taste was quite a shock to my system, but it reassured me that I was still on earth. Heaven would not be a place for tastes like this. I sat down by her feet and drank from the cold metal cup.

"You live here?" I asked, trying not to make it sound like an insult. But she did not answer. Nor did she seem to register any of my further question. Her name? Her parents? The name of the lake? She simply sat and occasionally looked very hard at my face then off across the lake where the gulls were fighting over an eel.

I felt disoriented by the way she was looking at me, partly because I now realized how pretty she was. She had long, straw-coloured hair that played in the slight breeze as if it had a life of its own. She was freckled and her eyes were soft brown. She had a way of sitting with her hands in her lap that I had never seen before in any girls I had ever known at school. But what was most unusual for me was the simple fact that I had never sat with a girl my own age, simply together, without speaking, without playing a practical joke on each other. This was something completely different.

I drew up the courage to look back directly into her eyes and she seemed to like that. She smiled at me for the first time.

Then she looked afraid. She went inside the shack and came back with a bowl of water and a cloth. My head had begun to bleed again. She dabbed gently at the wound and I tried to talk to her again but she still said nothing. When she was through, she tossed the water on the ground and went back inside. This time when she returned, she handed me a small printed card. It said simply, "I am a deaf mute. I can not always understand what you say but I am not stupid." The card was old and worn, like it had been handled many times in her life, explaining what others could not detect.

"I'm sorry," I said to her. "I'm so sorry."

Now she understood my message all too clearly. It was not what she wanted to hear. She was familiar with these words and I had deeply offended her. She now withdrew the card and pointed back toward the stream and the route that had led me here. I again tried to apologize, but it only seemed to make things worse. As I stood up, she pushed me away from the cabin and pointed away, showing me that I was no longer wanted.

I realized that I was about to lose something very valuable. Those few minutes sitting quietly with her had been unlike anything I had ever known. I wanted that feeling back again.

"Please," I begged her now. "Can I stay with you a little longer?" I pointed to the wound on my head.

She stopped shaking her arms at me. Then she looked at the ground. I had grown aware of the intensity of the sounds all around—the arguing of the gulls, the gentle song of the wind, but also the pounding of blood inside my head. I walked back toward her and held out my hand. I would have sacrificed the next ten years of my life if she had simply allowed me to touch her. But she turned and ran, not to her cabin but beyond it, into the forest. I knew I would only make things worse if I followed her. Instead, I walked back to where the stream siphoned the lake and I began my slow, painful walk toward the inlet and home.

* * *

I carried her gentleness and her isolation with me for a long time. Half a dozen times I had been tempted to hike back there again but always something very mundane and practical had diverted me. When I finally found the strength to avoid the practical, it was late summer. The stream had grown over with ferns and weeds and the air was thick with blackflies and mosquitoes. The stream itself had dried to almost nothing and there were dead fish lodged against broken boards that gathered to dam the trickle. A few of the deeper pools barely covered the large dark fish that I could not name. They were slow and unlike any creature I had ever seen as they allowed my hand to pick them up, then place them back again.

The lake itself was not nearly as far back into the woods as I had remembered. It had dried considerably so that it was reduced by about a third. The tarpaper shack was there, but the door was gone, summer hunters had riddled the sides with pellets and there was no sign of life around. Whoever had lived here was long gone. A metal cup was also shot up and lying on the ground with two dead, dried black beetles inside it. I sat by the cabin for a long time, feeling that I had been cheated out of something that I would maybe never find again. It was still and hot as the blackflies swarmed. I remained silent for a long time until I heard myself trying to sing something I had often heard Margaret sing when she was working alone, a wordless tune that seemed to express whatever it was I was feeling. Then I got up to follow the stream home again. It appeared worn out and lifeless to me now. The gaspereau would not return until the next spring and then, as the water surged back toward the sea, they would wrestle their way up to the lake and some would rediscover the place they had left the year before. Others would never make it that far and get caught by the gaspereau fishermen with the pitchforks who would heave them onto the flatbeds and haul them off to Halifax. It would not always be possible to reconfirm the truth.

_____Nowhere to be Found

Some days it can be an awful thing to be a young man trapped in the body of an old fool. One minute it's all so simple, the next, complex beyond confusion. I was not sure why my life had turned in the direction it had. If I was religious I might have called it a spiritual struggle. I wanted to meet all of my demons and my angels but lacked the patience to wait for death in order to have the confrontation.

Fasting seemed to allow me to move time around in fantastic new ways. Going from the past to the present and back was like walking into and out of different rooms. I only had to be careful that a draft didn't steal up and close the door behind me. I could walk around inside this temporal house almost at will and was comfortable in any room I had once occupied. I recognized the dangers, or at least I thought I did. But the rewards were too great to give it up. I would follow the stream to its source . . . much as I had done as a kid, when I wandered up the gaspereau brook to the house of the mute. When you are an old man, you have all the time in the world for the

excursions and if you tie one string tightly onto the doorknob
of the present, then unravel it as you go, you can always find
your way out.

I think it was a bout of melancholy that got me started on it.
Three days of sitting out damp, cold summer rains. Listening
to a radio. The Americans and the Russians, the people
starving in Africa, the stumblings of our own government, the
great extravagant efforts of so many intelligent men trying to
make black look like white and grey look like gold. Then Kelly
arrived one afternoon to tell me that she was hitchhiking to
Victoria with a young man from the Art School. (What had I
expected? That she would come live with an old skeleton on
a lonely cliff?) I lost four pigeons to the weasels before the
creatures were caught in a cage arranged as a trap. I walked
them to the highway, this pair of beautiful carnivores circling
each other behind wire. Then I flagged down Arnold Schi-
nicker who drives the big truck down East, supplying all the
little stores with Seven-Up and Orange Crush. Arnold said
he'd take the weasels as far as Tangier and let them go. I said
that was far enough. I trusted Arnold to do it. I had seen
Arnold pick up a turtle off the road once and set it off to one
side. And now my pigeons would be safe inside their rusty cars
for another few months until something else came along.

Maybe this is what happens when your biological clock tells
you it's about to stop ticking. This fasting, starving oneself for
the sake of the visions. If this was senility, then I wanted all of
it. The trick would be to hold onto just enough control, just
enough to slip in and out of time and place like I wanted to.
If I let go of the string, it would probably be that easy to let it
all go. But I had a good grip.

Kenzie found me once. He was lost inside the rum and I was
travelling through time and it must have been a hell of a
reunion. We both swore to Jesus we were both only twenty
years old again. He insisted I taste from his bottle and I knew
it'd half-kill me; I hadn't eaten for six days. But I sipped and
it went down like somebody shoving a burning coal down my
throat. Then my brain grew hot and quick all of a sudden.

Kenzie was going on and on about a frozen lake, even though this was the middle of July. He was remembering the summer that it never thawed. We had seen it together, although I didn't know him well back then. Kincaid and I had walked up and down lakes, axing the ice through here and there because somebody had convinced us that the only way we'd ever see a real summer was if we cut through the ice in enough places. If we could get the water to look straight up at the sky, that's all it would take. It was Joe Allen Joe who had convinced us of that. We'd have done anything for a real shot at summer that year. Joe himself stood at the edge of the ice, just where the lake waters met the saltier tides of the inlet, and he hacked away, working day and night sometimes. A good laugh the fishermen had over that. But even they were afraid something had gone wrong with the planet, something had frigged up somewhere, and we were all set for an ice age and bad fishing to boot. But Joe Allen Joe believed he had an inside edge. He too had talked of fasting in those days. I remember that now. As the only full-blooded Micmac around, he thought it was his duty to unstick the grip of the winter, even if the white men thought him a fool.

In the end, almost nothing worked. Ice held on hard in many places right on through to the new ice of fall. Kenzie remembered ice skating outside his backdoor in August and a cousin that had come down from Ontario, a pretty girl in a yellow dress with pigtails who had fallen on the ice and knocked herself out one day when he was skating with her. When she came back to consciousness, Kenzie was kissing her, figuring it might be the only shot he'd have at it in his life. She screamed so loud that Kenzie's old man shipped her all the way back to Kingston on the next train, confessing to his son later, "They don't know yet what kissing is in Ontario, son. You shoulda known better than that."

Kincaid and I gave up on chopping holes in the ice after a while. They'd skin over with ice like thin plate glass every night and somebody got word to us that one of the county councillors from up near the Head had fallen through in one of them, clean up to his shoulders. He was threatening to raise the taxes unless the culprits were surrendered. Not one of the fishermen would turn us in, though.

So Kenzie had no trouble with me that time, as we both could work in and around each other's minds since our lives had crossed at so many points before. After he had gone back home to his room that hadn't been swept since the early fifties, his leaky kettle that hissed away endlessly on his stove, and his true best friend, the Governor-General, I found my way back to the present and something inside me said that if I didn't eat tonight, I would die. It said that the second swig of rum I took on an empty stomach might just send me to sleep and never wake me up again. So I ate, and I slept, and I woke up disappointed to be living alone in the mundane present. But I was alive and much saner than I used to be.

The sun carved away the clouds and the pigeons were flying. I hadn't fed them for a couple of days and I was angry at my irresponsibility. Whatever I was doing to myself, I had not asked other living things to suffer in any way for it. So I went out and opened the feed can and spread the seeds around on the ground: cracked corn and wheat and rape seed and all those other tiny seeds of something or other. The birds flew down and circled me like a feathery tornado, spiralling down until they landed at my feet and began pecking at the ground. So I was fully back in the present. My knees and ankles ached the minor pains of old drying joints and my neck felt like it hadn't the strength to keep my head atop my shoulders. But inside, my brain sang the clear, bold song of the living. And when I went in to look at the calendar, for perhaps the first time in many days, I established what day of the week it was, and what date, and realized that it was the day I had been born. I was seventy years old and that was something right there.

* * *

None of us ever believe that we will get old and lose desire. At sixteen, sex and love are the most important forces in the world and the whole universe is a crazy, unrequited prison. Eventually we escape.

If it's only a biological clock, then it's just so much simple chemistry. I heard the man from the university say on the radio that none of us needed sex after all. It was just a sort of fad that caught on. Women could live without men and, given a few simple changes, they could reproduce all by themselves. Men were extraneous. The product of a fad. Thank goodness that a number of women had sort of grown used to us and kept us around. We're forever indebted to them for that.

Now I had learned that the need for food was also something frivolous. A few days' fasting and I was able to fine-tune time to go long or short for me. I had it very much under control. The poet's old complaint, resolved. That subtle thief reduced to no more than a pickpocket gathering lint. I could go backwards or forwards all I wished. Oh, mutable time, where is thy sting now? The trick was to be inside of it, inside of time. Usually we follow close to its heels and let it lead us. It takes us so long to learn things, a stubborn human race.

We live inside dream houses and forget to wash the windows. We look through dirty glass and can't make out the landscape. Until we are old.

I had to force myself to eat again. Caught up in a dream, inside of time. No, not a dream. Too real for that. Kincaid, the long lost, had returned in spirit to keep me company. We had little to say to each other but could recall feelings shared like noontime mackerel sandwiches cut in half. But I could not fully trust Kincaid; he still held the old grudge. If I wasn't careful, he would be very happy to trip me up and carry me down that tunnel to *his* side, the other side of life. Close-mouthed as usual, Kincaid owned up little as to what it was like there. He was satisfied with it, he would say, in a typical Eastern Shore fashion.

I was shocked at first to find the living as well as the dead inside the fasting visions. It was never the living of the present unless they actually arrived at my door greeting me as if I was a madman. Like the vacuum cleaner salesman the other day. I assumed that he too had come from my past, but he had instead pulled up in a Plymouth. He had no idea that anyone lived without electricity and that his Electrolux could be of no value to me. "It will suck us all to dust," I told him, me an old, senile prophet now. The man left me his card anyway, and retreated. Afterwards, I realized there was something about him that I liked. He was young and naïve, as we all should be. We have made a religion out of knowledge and wasted all our time in its accumulation. As I've said, though, time is retrievable. If you want it all back, just phone in your order.

* * *

Each time I get into it, I find it harder to relocate the desire for food. One day I might lose the desire for oxygen as well and then something will happen. My friend, the whale, this was his curse, or his blessing. Late one night last week, I broke myself free from the past by climbing down the hill again and walking out into the sea until the icy cool fingers gripped up my legs and grabbed at my testicles. I felt cold and pain and it alone burned me back to the living. I ate again, then slept, then cleaned out the pigeon cars and designed feeders to keep them better cared for than I could do these days that were carrying me away from their bright wings and toward those dark warm tunnels where most all things seemed possible. The living should never have to pay the debts of the near-dead.

Recently I was overcome with the desire to live for days at a time without sleep as well as without food. To see through the night head-on, to watch the sun set and the sun come up, merely by turning my chair around. And waiting. I did it three full days, then decided on a fourth without sleep and without food. I drank only water from the well. Maybe I was like the young kids who take drugs, wanting to see the world from the other side, wanting to break free from the muddied grip of reason. Maybe I expected more than I should have out of what was in front of me. I could have been crazy. It had been a long winter.

No one would bother me for days at a time and, lately, I wanted it like that. I thought of the old Inuit men and women drifting out to sea on chunks of ice. I would like to have felt the pride and loneliness that would go along with that. Was it a giving up to death, or an attempt to meet it head-on, a final confrontation? I was among them, not ready to go gentle into that good night, not willing to collapse into the waiting arms of some saviour. I wanted something more, simply to break down the barricades that separated the living from the dead. The more I studied the problem, the more reasonable it seemed.

I had already worked at it from this side: the whale, the education of Kincaid, and lately the dreams. But the dreams were beyond my control. I always lost out to the man at the switch, someone who wasn't within me. We let our dreams sweep over us. We can't touch those who need to be touched. The Indian, Joe Allen Joe, had taught me about dreams, about gaining control of them, about coaxing them to do what I wanted them to do.

I wanted, of course, all of the people back, all that I had lost, the living and the dead. My son was still alive, still somewhere hard at work carving out a life among the drones that called themselves the successful. All that striving, all that acquisition. I talked with him often on a borrowed phone and we had gained a new respect, but we were never communicating in the same language. Carey had lost the drive to kill himself, at least. He was happy, subdued, weakened in spirit somehow, and when I mentioned his former despair he would say, "I'm past all that now. It was just something I had to go through. You were right."

Jesus, I wasn't right about a thing. I would have been devastated had he succeeded in his Toronto death. So now he was half-alive, half-happy, all anyone could ask for, I suppose. I had given him my stubbornness, at least.

My love for my son would always be there, but he taught me that we're happier apart, living our own faulted lives, not bending to each other's will. The way it should be. If I could bring him back as a child we should get along famously, but it doesn't have to go that way.

And if I could steal Eleanor away from death and time, I knew she would have me back. It should all have been so simple, this matter of reunion. Then, too, I would call back my father and complete the story of his life myself, fill in the empty brackets from then to now, pour his life back into my early confused years, so vacant without him. It would be my father resurrected from his improbable maritime grave, who would understand most the means to negotiate with irrepressible fate. He would carry a grudge as large as mine and together we might go on, calling back all the lost souls to our hearts' content. Once begun, I was sure the arrogant meddling of the past could be brought to account for itself within the present. And the future would be a false notion altogether.

Why is it, that at seventy, one becomes consumed by the young man inside his chest that wants to live it all over again? Time has never been fair. All those old poets arguing with time, bitching away at time's indifferent back: Milton, Donne, Marvell, Shelley, Keats. On and on. *Carpe diem,* yes! The only Latin I know. But it's not good enough to seize the day; the poet in us all needs to get inside of time, pump ourselves like fresh, alien blood into the veins of time and arrest the muscle if need be. To kill time ultimately and become alive without it.

I want you to see what I saw first while looking deep into the grain of the grey, weathered planks of the wall. Age had brought out the silver in these once golden boards of pine. They now looked like an old man's silvered hair. There was order, control, seasons with and without rain that had carved a fresco here. The life of a tree, dried up and gone from its ribs years ago, and still something of beauty left here. I remember the rip of the handsaw across the plank that was a tree and how I had helped form it into a wall and how I had lived with that wall all these years. There was a special link between me and it. And now I was sitting in a hardbacked maple chair staring into it like I was reading a book and I was grateful to it for helping me snap the locks inside my brain, undo the damages of time. In the shoot-out, I was sure, we were all capable of perfect memory.

* * *

It's so simple that it almost seems a waste of breath to say it all again, but the truth has been out for a long time and it hasn't been enough. I had found the place I was looking for, the rented room outside of time, a place at the centre of my life when I was young and in love and discovering a means to get control of it all. Eleanor was there with me and we were building this house, both working together, stopping for nothing less than to make love on the warm summer grass.

I could feel the power of that time strong enough inside of me so that I knew she was again there with me. We were filled with a million reasons to be alive. Eleanor. How could so much life be tied to one person? And what cruel powers would decide to rob me of her? I felt the anger welling up. The desire to kick death in the teeth. My anger brought a fearsome darkness into the room. It had been night all along. I knew that now. The light had come from within and so had Eleanor. Now this. Cold, dark, something wanting to fight back at me, to tell me that there was a price to be exacted for the act of displacing time. But I struggled against it even as I felt something like cold claws around my neck, then around my chest, something tightening and not wanting to let go until I gave in. My anger made the constriction worse. Before me on the table, I knew, were matches and a candle. The blackness was still all around but I could feel my way with my hands and as I did, I fought off my own hatred. The match was struck and the candle lit and I was again looking deep into the grain of the bare wood, turned back from silver to gold now in the warm flame of the candle.

Then the panic inside was gone and Eleanor was again with me. Not the young Eleanor, but the woman who died in my arms, older, tired, human. As she died before me a second time, I looked deep into her eyes and saw that the flame within her continued to burn. And again, I was content to be an old man sitting alone in an empty room on the edge of a cold continent. The world was moving along at its usual impossible speed all around me. And I was nowhere to be found.

twisting

black into white
grey into gold — mundane
mind

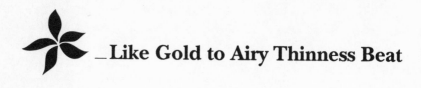

Like Gold to Airy Thinness Beat

West is sunset and west is death. In the cool evenings now I lean into the setting sun, I press my cheeks against the west window and feel as clear as glass. The sun sings through me. It burns red, a dying ember inside my chest and I am happy to say that this has been a life. Each man must say it to himself: it was mine. I lived it, I was nothing other than what I am. And thankful that it was not a life lived alone. Here on this shore where people try to separate themselves from other living things, I was not among the cursed ones who lived alone. I found and I kept and when time came and tore it away from me, I lingered. I fight and grieve and would gladly tear out the heart of any living god who felt he had the right to claim what was mine, but I linger, I do not give in.

Look west and what's there? It's good that death should be west of here. The poets have all found it so. I have read them, God knows why. Even now in my old age they speak to me in my sanctuary of dreams and loneliness and perfect, holy fits of vision and longing. Eleanor and I read Wordsworth together, and Donne ("westward, westward") and even Alfred Lord Tennyson knew my sea from the other side. It was often like staring into a crazy mirror. And later, Kelly gave me Whitman, that crazy Yank, if only they all had been like him, alive, kicking at the throat of all the zealots who wanted to turn democracy into tyranny. If only he was alive today in America, chanting in the streets, cataloguing the vital extravagance of life and vindictive of all the destructive weapons of our imaginations. ("Unscrew the doors from their jambs!") Even Kenzie arrives on a moonless night spilling Robbie Burns into the stars—"That Man to Man thae warld o'er, / Shall brothers be for a' that."

And west is west and east is east. The twain meet here. Outside my window at sunset. Inland and west, the continent grows heavy with the weight of greed, of progress, of fear and mistrust. I feel it sinking, a lead heart beneath an empty, rotted sky. They came here first, the Europeans, weighted down with God and power and desire. They found this coast first and here in the north it was cold, unforgiving but beautiful. Some stayed and died. Some stayed and killed—the Beothuk, the Micmac, the coastal peoples who knew enough of the ways of the sea to back off when winter came.

And then God swept his hand and the settlers passed on— south and west carrying much of the corruption with them. A few of us stayed in places like this with the cold and the clean and the hard blue line of sea keeping us honest. Soon the sad, starved people came here and called it home, or called it at least enough—the Highlanders, the Irish, the French, who were not wanted on their own streets. And history did the same to us as it did to all the rest, but after a while it forgot us and soon we were a land of old men staring off into sunsets, wishing again for the sight of canvas knives scoring the horizon.

Thank God someone opened the floodgates here in this dominion and allowed the trade to flow off to Montreal and Toronto like unwanted sediment. If this is poverty, then this is bliss. Yet can a man fight to keep it so? It is not possible.

* * *

Sibility—I want all of it

Carey arrived without advance notice, last week. He complained of the ruts in the road and his new wife tried to pretend she liked me, but I could see what she saw from behind those cold blue eyes: an old crazy man, a man needing an asylum, a man gone over the hill of life and trapped in a mad valley of demons and spirits. Poor Carey, sad Carey. The love in my heart for the little boy in him was hard enough to find. The boy was still there inside all those adult clothes, behind those frantic eyes. Carey, always searching, always restless as any boy should be, but always so hopeful of immediate salvation that he grabbed from ring to ring until he reached for air and emptiness.

"Things are fine now," he said to me. He meant that he was no longer trying to undo his life with pills or razors.

"Carey and I have a wonderful life," his missus said. I could see that she meant it although the truth was elastic. "We want you to come live near us in Toronto."

"Near?" I heard myself say, sounding like the old grizzly they saw me to be.

"A community of golden agers." The words came from Carey but they were not his.

"What am I, some frigging pedigree dog?"

"You need proper care," the missus insisted. She saw me as an old man who sat around with pee stains on his pants, an unshaven refugee, a victim of age and malnutrition. Who was I to prove her otherwise?

The sun was out, but it began to rain. I have always enjoyed that minor miracle, easy enough to understand, but a miracle all the same. The wind blowing water miles perhaps from clouds too distant to see, that's all. Each drop fell like warm diamonds on my face.

"We should go inside before we catch pneumonia," Carey said, a man now of responsibility. I remembered when Eleanor and I had nursed *him* through pneumonia. He had not caught it from a sunshine shower but from the hospital where he had gone to have his tonsils out. His mother and I sat up through many nights just listening to our boy breathe, warding off anything else the hospital was offering up to kill him.

"Dad, we want to see that you have proper care and that you're near us. Now that . . . she . . . is gone, you need someone."

"I need, yes, but not what you think." They were looking around the old house now, just standing there, staring like they had been dropped into some medieval chamber of horrors.

"I need to use the bathroom," the woman said. We had not yet even been properly introduced. I didn't know her name. God what a terrible son Carey had become! What an awful, senile old goat of a father I must have seemed to him! Here we were, staring down each other in purgatory.

"It's outside. Go left, you can't miss it." Poor girl turned white, held her kidneys, I guess, rather pee inside the grimy walls of some gas station restroom, just as long as the toilet pulls a flush. "But you can just go anywhere in the woods, it's okay with me," I added. Instead she sat down at the table.

"We were thinking we could sell the land. I already talked to a developer in Halifax and he believes in this property."

"Goddamn, son. *Believes* in it?"

"He can subdivide, make mini-estates. Sell them to the oil people, the West Germans, the Americans maybe." Honest ambition and hope in this voice, the voice of my own son. The voice that thinks of land as a piece of real estate. So it can be undone. You can be born here, raised here, feel the veins in your blood fill up with salt from the sea and minerals from this very plot, then drive off to an inland city and learn that it was nothing more than real estate. All this in the blink of an eye. I said none of it.

"Americans, West Germans?"

"With the money, Carey and I can take care of you, have you properly taken care of. You shouldn't live here like this."

"Like what?"

Her truthful answer was slow to come out and, in the end, she lied . . . "Alone."

It amazes me to think that what I felt for them both was pure, unmitigated hate. Had I spoken too quickly, they might have sent off for men and strait-jackets. I might have been lost forever. I understand that here in Canada, you only need a doctor, maybe it's two, to say that you are incompetent. Then it's all over, you lose your freedom. I turned away from them, though. I fired all that hate into the wall. It stood well, lost nothing. This is a good house. I've given it lots of anger and hate before and it's never come back on me. Those upright walls of wood placed lovingly together by Eleanor and me could absorb it all. So much love went into this place that it would withstand anything. Go ahead, drop that righteous bomb on me instead of Halifax, see if the structure would hold.

If Carey's wife had seen my eyes then, she would have run for the rented car, locked the doors, turned on the radio and closed her own eyes. But when I turned around, I had swallowed it all up. I had wrapped it carefully back into my life, into my memory of who this younger man was and who he had been. And I knew as well that he was the product of Eleanor and me and the world and one of the three of us had not fully done our work. And maybe I was to blame or maybe not. It mattered little.

"I'll make some tea," I said and smiled. "Then I'll make us some food." I said nothing more about the proposals. Two fighter jets flew over then, red wingtips carving away at the sky. The sound crashed inside the room and was gone. When I got up to look out the window, I saw the rainbow there in the north and the sun leaning almost as far south as west. Before the light was gone from the sky, Carey remembered who he had once been and relocated the land that was still inside him and I could even see that his wife understood. We climbed down to the base of the cliff and sat in the sunset and I told them about saving the whale, about my pigeons, about the summer that never happened and more. When it was time for them to

leave, it was Carey's wife, her name I had learned was Annie,
who said to me, "We understand now and we both love you
very much." Carey had already started up the car, but I knew
it was him talking to me as well as Annie. It was probably my
fault I had never taught him to express his emotions. Men, in
my day, were lousy teachers. They could teach a boy to hoe,
to mend nets, to build barns or fix engines, but they couldn't
teach a boy to say what he felt. I had really botched that one.

Carey did roll down the window of the car as I walked over
to say a last goodbye to him, and I knew it would be the final
one. We shook hands. Men could do that. I looked deep in
his eyes and saw the me in him. The uncertainty of the younger
man, the fears, the inabilities, but a will to get on with it. He
nearly cracked the bones in an old man's wrist.

When their tail-lights had faded from the driveway, and the
east was given back to green and black, I went back to the
window and watched the last soft glow of red that ringed the
land beyond Halifax—Sambro Light ticked a white flash every
minute—as I gathered the fading sun inside my chest and felt
it warm against my ribs as it dreamed me back into myself.

* * *

I gave up on the fasting for a while, worried that Death was
out there to trick me after all, to trip me up in my own madness
and steal in through the window without my knowing it. I
could still eat but had lost a great deal of the will to want to
do it. Desire. When you're young, you never believe you will
lose the hunger for food, the demand for sex, or the thirst for
booze. Maybe some don't. Maybe some are glad to lose the
drive for it. To me, it's just a surprise, that's all.

Summer sometimes doesn't really make itself comfortable
in Nova Scotia until September and this year, September was
summer's favoured month. I went out to my garden and saw
how I had neglected it, let the weeds tower over the beans, let
the lettuce go to seed. It didn't seem to matter to me before,
but now it was a demand. I picked up my hoe and planned to
bring order back to the wilderness. There was a strong ache
inside me, something that wanted to ignore all this and get

back to the things I could do with my mind. As I began to hoe out the pigweed, I thought about what I had been up to. Was it just the learned ability to hallucinate, or something more than that? It wasn't just a clever, inexpensive way to entertain myself without a television set. I wasn't convinced that it was all made up, that it was the conjuring of a senile old fart. Sure as the devil, the younger world would not tell me it was a sane thing to do, or that I was making contact with other levels of existence. I wouldn't try to convince anyone of that anyway. But it was the power that gave me back my life, the past and the present, and I was free to move around within a realm more satisfying than what this other, mundane world had left me. And I would leave it at that.

A faint morning mist was now lifting, leaving a damp, warm land to dry out beneath the late summer sun. I could feel it pulling the sweat up through my skin and it felt very good. Even the sourness of my own unwashed self smelled good to me, for smell is a strong drug that also retrieves the past and it reminded me of the afternoons Eleanor and I had worked here on this plot of soil, removing the rocks, wondering at how they grew back like hard potatoes, almost day by day, throughout the summer.

The rocks had grown back this year with abandon. I had not been around to play their games and the garden was theirs, shared with the pigweed, the chickweed, the miner's lettuce, couch-grass and wild camomile. I'd be hard-pressed to find the beets and parsnips, the turnips and cabbage for winter storage. If I had to, I'd live out of cans this winter.

I unbent my back, feeling the years gathering revenge in my spine. Nothing like a hoe to make a man feel old and crooked. Then I turned around and saw that I was nearly face to face with a heron. It had landed behind me in absolute silence and stood there, not four feet away, among the broken weeds and brown peas. It did not move, nor did I. This blue heron, like all others I had ever seen, possessed grace, power and beauty unlike any other bird or creature alive. I had watched them for years in the shallows by the inlet and at the marshes of

Lawrencetown and Chezzetcook, but I had never seen one up on land, in a man's garden like this. I wondered if my visionary quest had reached beyond the fast, if the bird was here as a manifestation of something still wandering in my mind.

That bold spear of a head, the needle-like orange bill and a neck like a powerful weapon, cocked and ready to fire. I had seen her, or others like her, stand in infinite patience on a foggy pond, legs invisible, hanging like a wraith in mid-air, motionless for hours at a take, then darting the neck into the glassy water and pulling out an eel as long as its own length, before swallowing it whole. And when it flew, you could see that the wings carried it with such ease that perhaps the body had no weight at all. On a grey day, it could make itself invi-sible in the wink of an eye, that silver-grey frame dissolving in the air, or pulling itself up into the clouds with one incandescent flap of wings, then landing again in the shallows like a gentle kite pulled in by a gossamer thread from beneath the eelgrass.

She walked around, not toward me. I flashed again on what I had seen as a child, fresh out of Halifax, sitting in Margaret's hot kitchen reading a book about dinosaurs to get my mind off the loss of my mother, the confusion of my father. I remember going out to the inlet and watching one land before me—a pterodactyl, alive and living on the Eastern Shore. How Margaret had laughed at me for that. When I later told my father, he asked first what a pterodactyl was and when I explained, he looked at me hard and sad, no humour in his face, then he pulled me to him again and scraped his rough chin across my face until I thought I would bleed.

Joe Allen Joe had explained the Great Blue Heron to me as well. He had no trouble convincing me that they were his dead relatives. "They return, you know," he said. "I have never lost a relative who does not return. Some come back as snakes. This does not surprise me. But the ones I loved always return as Greywings." I let him lead me inland to the little ponds set in the notches of the coastal hills, places where gulls and ducks gathered and herons as well. He had names for the birds in each landlocked lake. "You can talk to them from along the shore. They hear you and remember who you are, but you should not go too close. They have already travelled a great distance to come back to your land and you should give them plenty of room." But Joe enjoyed being in their company, to be again with great-uncles and cousins. He would never let us get too close or try to feed them. Once or twice he tried to teach me to speak their language, and I was frightened by the curious sound that he could make in his throat. The herons would answer him and once it so frightened me that I ran off through the forest, almost losing myself once more in a thick wilderness of stunted spruce and fog until I reached the edge of the headland where the broken trees fell off the banks of the drumlin down the dirt cliffs to the sea. Then I followed the coast home as I had often done. I couldn't count the number of times I had become lost as a child growing up here. Always I had found some mechanism to lead me to the coastline, then my way home would be clear. A man is never lost if he knows where the land ends and the sea begins.

So, at first, I left the garden heron alone and continued hoeing, believing it would remain if I didn't try too hard to make contact, She walked a close arc around me and I watched her as I worked. When she had almost completed the circumference I saw her other side and realized she was having trouble keeping one wing up. It drooped as she tried to draw it up on her back until finally it fell and trailed on the ground. There was dried blood upon the lavender grey and I felt cheated out of my small miracle. I knew why the heron was here in this unlikely place. It had settled here with me because she too was about to die. Damn!

I walked over to my shed and, still pretending to ignore the bird who stood like an ornament now among the broken weeds, I found a section of fishing net that had washed in. Returning to the garden, I found her standing on one foot, an eye half-closed, but quick to regain her footing and grow fully awake as I approached. I closed my own eyes, centred on where she was, then without opening them, heaved the polypropylene net out and over her in one quick move. She let out a shriek and nearly escaped but I gathered the edges of the net and held her still.

Fearful of choking her or doing more damage to the wing, I quickly untangled the bird, wishing I had worn heavy leather gloves and a helmet for I was certain it was ready to spear out my eyes. I had to brace the neck like someone holding back a snake and I also had to arrest the flapping wing. She weighed almost nothing. All feathers and spirit, as Joe Allen had said, nothing more. But the power in her neck and feet was tremendous and when she finally grabbed onto my hand with her beak, I thought she would cut clean through. I let her hold on though, and as her feet dug deep into my thighs and the beak clamped down on my hand like a rattlesnake, I eased her out of the net and into the house. For the world, as I had always known, was often in need of repair and usually against its own will.

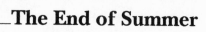

The End of Summer

I was beginning to worry—here's the old man in me again—that life *doesn't* work in cycles. Seasons were so convincing. They usually reappeared. Yet even there the cycle could be snapped. That improbable summer where summer never arrived stayed with me. What if some folks' lives were like that? One cold, hard winter. But what I was getting at was a new fear that life was, well, linear. It begins here, ends there and that's it, an old rutted dirt road coming to a blank stop in the middle of a forsaken swamp.

Maybe, maybe not. See, you can't help thinking about all the people in your life when you crank up the years this far. It's like an old Ford with a high idle and maybe lousy timing: once she's running, you can't get her to stop even after you turn off the key. I thought for a short while that I had lost them all, but they all returned again. I could go with or without the food. Now that I had the tricks down, all I needed was a good stretch of being alone and I could remember them all just as I'd like to. Fool that I was, I never even saved snapshots.

Instead, I relied on a Kodak brain. I didn't talk to them anymore, these people from the past, I just felt warm in their company.

Kenzie, the real Kenzie, kept coming by once in a while to interrupt things, but I didn't mind. And Nora came by to cook me a meal for no good reason that I can see. I could hardly talk to either of them. They all wanted to know about the heron. Well, she seemed to be coming along. I taped that wing with a splint and fed her on Millionaire Sardines, which seemed to bring no objection. It would take her four weeks before she might fly again, and I knew she'd be capable when the time arrived. If she was the spirit of somebody, she found herself in a curious limbo, living inside somebody's old car with chicken wire where the glass used to be. And I expected something would happen when it was time to set her free. Who was it that had come back to visit me, anyhow? Eleanor? Muriel, who might yet be living or dead for we had lost touch? Not that we had ever really talked . . . but Muriel had been there for a long time, all evil and beauty and truth and corruption, all tied up into one knot of human injury. And Margaret had grown away from me as I grew old. She had moved in with one man, then another, as each moved on or died. She had always been available in a soft, caring way for all who needed her. A saint, perhaps the only one we ever had on the Eastern Shore. The great silver bird was someone coming back around to complete the cycle, Joe Allen Joe would assure me of that. Maybe it was Joe himself, although that seemed wrong since the bird seemed so feminine despite the anger and fight it gave me in trying to save its life. That's the way it works, you know: we always fight and try to destroy the ones who try to save us. Compassion is sometimes a cruel thing to the victim. *not Eleanor*

I don't mind. I've done some clawing and biting in my time. Maybe the victims are right. Look at the world. How many of the leaders tell us that they want to build the next killer weapon, the next impossible tool for destruction so that they can save us? Maybe compassion is among the deadliest of emotions. But for me, it's all I've got. The summer will soon be gone.

* * *

I heard from Carey again. A letter. He and his new wife were going to have a baby. If it turned out a boy they'd name it for me. There's love in that somewhere and there's also love in the fact that he allowed me to stay here, left me alone. Not that I would have gone anywhere, mind you. It's just kind of him that he gave up. Leaving people alone is where the real compassion is.

I haven't been sleeping much these days. The north winds have been coming back and I go out at night beneath the clear, open sky and study the Milky Way until I see that it is filled with cold, bright angels. They shout out their names and I say nothing back. I've heard my heron sing too, if singing it is. She knew her time was about up in the cage. Four weeks. The wings would have to be freed and her flight tested. Much more and she'd rot in that metal cave. A bird like that was not meant to spend the end of her days staring into the eyes of a dead six-volt radio.

That sound she made was enough to chase the devil from this coast, lonesome and angry and sad, all tied up into one note that cracked against a morning sky. She had nothing to complain about on one level: I'd been feeding her good, better than myself. Once more I was feeling that the need to eat had evaporated.

But you have to realize that I wasn't mad. I was what I wanted to be and I wasn't satisfied to leave the rest of life alone. I had to invite it all back in for a visit now and again and I can't see a thing wrong with that. I fixed up the pigeon pens so that the birds could all go in and out as they pleased without fear of cats or weasels or foxes. And even my poor old garden, all yellowed and going to seed, would be good food for the lot of them if I became lazy or something else happened.

And I was surprised to be seeing angels up in the sky for I never understood exactly what role they played and, to tell you the truth, I didn't trust them one bit, nothing of what they were saying. But I sat out with them on a number of occasions just to make them feel like I was being polite. Finally, one pulled down close and I knew her to be the mute girl I had found once at the end of the gaspereau stream. She put her hand on my forehead again and it was cool and peaceful until there was pain there too, the pain I had felt when I had fallen and cracked my head open that day long ago. Then she pulled her hand away and the pain was gone. She was gone too, but in her place was a woman I didn't recognize at first. It was my mother, her memory salvaged from deep down in the wreckage of my early childhood. And if I could have just kept staring up into the night sky, I'm sure I would have been folded into her arms and drawn up into her warm smile. I felt her hair falling now about my own shoulders.

But as soon as she was gone, I felt hollow and cheated. I was destroying myself in my own games. I had succeeded in breaking down the barriers I so detested between the past and the present, between those alive and those long gone. It was completely within my will now and very easy. But it was not enough. It wasn't life. Dark clouds were scudding in from the north, burying the galaxy behind them and turning the night sour and bitter. I went inside determined to sleep.

Instead, I lay there all night in a cold sweat, hearing the insis-tent voice of the heron. She would have to be freed now. Her other life was coming; she would change continents, wise enough to avoid sticking it out here for the winter. She would want none of winter and would be driven by greater life forces than I understood to do as she was designed. My own anger was building in me, ricocheting back from before my days of conjuring. The sea began to slap at the bottom of the cliffs, taunting me, wanting something from my own turmoil. I could feel it again in my blood, not as I had felt it as a boy but in a new way. It was there, pulsing with a restless power and confused energy that would have to loose itself in the depths or thrash itself out against some headland. It was devoid of face or form and I felt again the pain and loss of Eleanor. She alone had kept me sane. And now she was gone for good. I could no longer believe in my powers to merge past and present. It wasn't good enough anymore. I had pushed it to the limit and had seen it to be no more than a game, a sort of television set for those without electricity and a metal antenna.

Had I the will right then to get up, I would have torched the house and wandered off into the empty night. And that would have been the end of it. But I was paralyzed. The muscles had been removed from my body and I was nothing more than a bag of skin, bones and blood. Then suddenly the sun was there at the east windows. The wind had stopped but the anger burned on in me. It had found a new focus and the target was my father. My father who had plowed the seas and left his son to make his own way. My father who had saved my own life once with a hunch, but had not been willing to save my mother as well. How could he have done that?

My body found itself again. I was up out of bed, almost insulted to find it had turned into a gentle, warm and bright fall day, the last trickster day of summer before the cold clammy onslaught. The heron croaked her ragged song and I took a knife and went out to her. She was very still now as I held her in my arms and put my fingers around the impossibly thin neck, feeling the pulse of the creature and looking into its face and seeing nothing at all but the face of another living thing, programmed to fly here or there, genetically trained to stand in pools and spear other living things in order to live. And I saw how I had been programmed to do the same. To survive, to suffer, to cause others pain.

I pulled in on the neck ever so gently and with my right hand slit the cloth tape that had held the broken wing fixed in place. The splint fell free from the wing and I looked at the wound. It had healed. The bone appeared to have mended and that brought momentary reprieve from my private grief. I walked the heron down the cliffs to the sea and gently placed her in the shallows. She fell over sideways, those thin erector-set legs collapsing beneath her. But as she toppled, she splashed with her wings, both spreading out wide like palm branches over the blue, calm waters. She tempted the air twice, then pulled down hard on them and leaned forward, barely moving, but at last edging forward and releasing the locks of gravity. She flew, at first just inches from the water, then catching a light updraft near the cliffs, up, circling higher and higher until I lost her in the sun and there was just a rippled shadow upon the sea. And with one final croak, she was gone.

There was one more sling yet to be undone. I took off my shirt and edged into the sea, gingerly stepping over the mussel-crowded rocks, the sea urchins and the barnacles. I took off my shoes and my pants, lay down among the flowing seaweed and began to swim. It was cold but not impossible. Nothing like the arctic waste I had once thrown Kincaid into, the sea that could fool physics into keeping water liquid far below the freezing point of any planet. Now the early October sea was cool but lacking the grip of real cold.

I swam out away from the headland that was my home and as I swam, looked down, searching the bottom for the unlikely destination. If Burchell had been telling the truth, I would find it out here, somewhere in the small bay between my cliff and the abbreviated hill that was known as Wedge Island. I had time and patience and all the energy in the world. For he had failed to find me on his return and I would have one last chance to find him and hold onto him forever.

The bottom was alive with lobster and crab and hypnotic flowing weeds that covered the rocky bottom. There was no sand out here and the view below was clear and clean. Everything was alive—fish swam around me, oblivious to my intrusion. I avoided a Portuguese man-of-war who had drifted up in the Gulf Stream. Off toward the horizon, I could see an oil rig being towed toward the Banks. Tankers and Coast Guard ships drifted farther out. But my main interest was below. I could swim the surface looking down and go for long periods of time without breathing. I realized suddenly that oxygen was like sleep or food or sex. You could live without it. It was all a matter of mind. But I wasn't ready for that move yet.

I searched for perhaps an hour, not tiring at all, almost gaining strength from my slow, persistent search. Even this far from shore the water was a mere twelve to twenty feet deep. The visibility perfect. And then I found what I had been looking for.

The plane was sitting on the bottom, a heap of rust grown over in seaweed, nothing easily distinguishable as an airplane, but something out of place here, something man-made. I took a deep breath and went down. I had found him at last. First, I slid along the wing until I found the opening, a two-seat cockpit barely discernible as anything other than a comfortable metal grotto for sea creatures. The glass was gone and the opening just wide enough to climb in. He was still there, a skull, a ribcage, sitting upright in the seat. He was still strapped in, what was left of him. One hand had been cut off at the wrist. But they had left his bones. History had less interest in them. The teeth were still there, in place in the skull. My father had always been proud of his teeth. He had cleaned them with cakes of salt that made his gums red, but his teeth white. They were still white and perfect.

What I was feeling was nothing I could pin down. Certainly not relief. And the hate, the anger at him for leaving me was almost gone, but I was filled with a feeling of revenge, and perhaps pity for myself. So many people had left me alone in my life and still I had survived. I had gone on to feel the pain that they were free to leave behind. It hadn't been fair. And now was my chance at reversing all that.

I put my arm around my father and I held on tight. I knew that I could sit there for as long as I wished. My desire, my need for oxygen was gone. I felt a slight burning in my chest but nothing more. All I had to do was hold on. And I held. As I looked up at the sky above the sea, I saw how beautiful it was from down here, looking up from beneath an ocean splayed out beneath the sea of air. We had missed so much in our life up above, the patterns of light dancing upon water viewed from below. I wanted to tell my father I was here. I wanted him

to know how much it had hurt and I wanted him to feel with
me the loss of Eleanor as if it was his own loss of my mother
that he could have stopped.

The world would have no dominion over me again. I had
been training well. Man did not need to live in the sea of air
at all. He could survive below like this forever if he liked. A
warm dark feeling began to seep into my thoughts and when
I could locate it, I began to grab onto it. There was colour
there—first dark blue, then red, then black, but behind it a
golden yellow light that was filled with faces, many faces but
all blending into one and I felt so happy that I was moving
toward them.

But suddenly I heard a low, monstrous explosion. It pulled
me back through the spectrum and I wanted to rage at the
source. A sharp pain rose up in my chest and I wanted to
scream, to breathe in water, to crush the pile of bones that was
beside me. A giant dark form moved up along the side of me
and circled the carcass of the plane. I saw some sea creature's
giant tail above the water's surface, blotting out the sun then
slamming down hard on the water with a second crushing
explosion. Then reason left me and panic set in. I heaved
myself out of the seat and jammed my knuckles into the frame
as I pushed for the surface and for air.

* * *

I remember pain and fear and splashing frantic panic that
twisted itself into exhaustion then back into aching lungs and
worn-out muscles that decided to continue working of their
own accord until I had found a place where the sea gave way
to a small beach of black sand notched into the dirt cliffs. And
sleep was a place without dreams or faces and when I awoke I
was filled with the ache to live, to breathe, to eat and, again,
to remember. As I closed my eyes I felt Eleanor all around me
and when I opened them she was gone. And that was enough.
If I leaned up on one elbow, I could see my house farther along
the headland perched like a foolish toy near the precipice.
Above it I saw my pigeons spiral in and then out again as if
they were a single living wing. And as I studied the hill and the

house and the birds, it occurred to me that back there was a very satisfactory place for an old man to live out the rest of his life, that a short walk over some slippery stones, and a steep hike up a path would get him there soon enough. And that once he got there, he might sit himself down to a cup of tea and a tin of sardines and that it might not be so bad. A man could maybe even handle that.

distance
detached

social.

existential freedom

even death was imagination
physical law - imagination
ignore it in mind → not crazy
just control